Waters That Drown Us

Rae Douglas

To everyone who picked up this book solely because of the phrase "sapphic CNC on a boat". You get it.

And to Erica and Cas. For making my music taste so much gayer.

Trigger and Content Warnings

Trigger Warnings
  Stalking
  Kidnapping
  Parental abuse (non-sexual)
  Murder
  Torture
  Blood
  Deception between love interests

Explicit Sexual Themes
  Dom/Sub Dynamics
  Pleasure Dom/Brat Dynamics
  Consensual non-consent (CNC)
  Consensual non-consent (CNC) on a boat
  Edge Play
  Bondage
  Fear Play

This book is a work of fiction and should be treated as such. While mega horny and mega hot, this book contains a *lot* of unhealthy representation of kink. This romance book (like all others) should act as inspiration, not education. If you're inspired by any of the activities Emily and Alice explore, please seek out educational resources on risk aware consensual kink (RACK).

Pronunciation, Definition, and Translation Guide

Definitions

- Class II Vessel: Boats measuring between 26 and 40 feet.
- Class III Vessel: Boats measuring between 41 and 65 feet.
- Cnidarians: aquatic invertebrates including jellyfish, sea anemones, corals, and marine parasites. All of these animals have barbed structures called nematocysts that are used to "sting" and capture prey.
- Mariinsky: A Russian ballet, one of the world's leading companies.

Translations & Pronunciations

- звездный свет. Language: Russian. Pronunciation: zvezdnyy svet. Translation: starlight.

- **Дядя**. Language: Russian. Pronunciation: Dyadya. Translation: Uncle.
- **Медуза**. Language: Russian. Pronunciation: Medusa. Translation: Jellyfish.
- **Назвался груздем - полезай в кузов.** Language: Russian. Pronunciation: Nazvalsya gruzdem - polezay v kuzov. Translation: If you call yourself a mushroom, climb in the basket. Equivalent to the English *in for a penny, in for a pound*.
- **Черт**. Language: Russian. Pronunciation: Chert. Translation: A curse like *hell* or *fuck*.
- **クラゲ**. Language: Japanese. Pronunciation: Kurage. Translation: Jellyfish.

COSTA FAMILY TREE

Playlist

You - Greta Isaac
Nothing's Gonna Hurt You Baby - Cigarettes After Sex
Corset - Azee
The Antidote - St. Vincent
RIP KP - King Princess
Keep On Coming - Gia Woods
Touch - Kehlani
Boyfriend - Dove Cameron
Talk - Hozier
willow - Taylor Swift
band practice - Ambré
talk you through it (feat. FLO) - kwn, FLO

Prologue
Emily

Twelve Years Ago

I shouldn't be here.

Actually, it might be *illegal* for me to be here. Certainly ill-advised.

Zia Lucia has been in tentative talks with an up-and-coming arms dealer out of Vladivostok, determining if his ambition can be used to our advantage. Clara and Charlie, both newly eighteen with real Syndicate responsibilities, are off on some recruiting mission in the Yukon. And Zio Aurelio is recovering from having his appendix removed. So I was tapped as my aunt's plus-one for this very long weekend. It's supposed to be an easy job, even for an infamously hardheaded and rebellious teenager such as myself. I'm to attend meetings with my aunt, be silent and observant, make pleasant conversation when approached, and not leave our secure accommodations after dark.

And I have followed all the rules.

Except that last one.

But I heard a rumor that our host's daughter is also sneaking out tonight. And that's something I can't miss.

I sit on the darkened balcony, listening to the hum of conversation as the lights flicker overhead. No one looks at me too closely, but I still readjust the scarf hiding my face. I'm not the only one obscuring my identity, so acting suspicious ironically makes me blend in. It's not like we're at the fucking Mariinsky.

My Russian isn't great, but I knew enough to navigate to the wine bar above us, slip a small roll of bills and the right phrase—**звездный свет**—to the sommelier, and find my way underground to this well-worn seat. And as the light fades, I pick up a few whispered words here and there. Whispers about *her*.

It's too dark to see the curtain rise, but I hear it. Slow and creaking, like the hull of a boat in unfriendly seas. And when it quiets, a single spotlight illuminates what can only be described as an angel.

She stands center stage, draped in iridescent organza—her entire existence seeming like a mirage. White-blonde hair falls down her back, frizzing strands catching in the harsh overhead light, creating a soft halo around her. Fresh flower petals adorn her hair, her skin, her dress—as though scattered by the wind or some unseen deity. A carefully painted mask of red, orange, and lilac obscures her features, but I would know that face anywhere. I've stared at her for so many hours this weekend, I could probably draw her from memory alone, and I'm no artist. She lifts the viola to rest beneath her chin as more sunset-hued petals scatter from the folds of her dress to create a garden at her feet.

An angel.

The audience holds their breath, the silence surrounding

me almost oppressive as we wait for her to pull the bow across the strings.

When the music finally comes, it's perfect. There's no other word that fits. The fragility of the sound—like each note might shatter under the weight of its own beauty—keeps our breath caught in our chests. I don't pretend to have a great understanding of classical music, especially not *Russian* classical music, but I am decidedly converted. The movement she plays expands my understanding of sound, painting a picture in the air. Of running, of fingertips skimming cascading waves, of droplets on skin and eyes closing against the wind.

But even the elegance of her music can't compete with what it is to look at her. Her body sways, shoulders dipping and brow furrowing as she pulls the bow across the strings over and over again. It reminds me of videos my father showed me of Mercedes Sosa, the way every molecule of her body was consumed by the music she sang.

The sound changes, and so does her energy. In my mind's eye, the picture she paints is still of someone running, but no longer only to feel the Earth under their feet or the wind against their face. Now, they're running *from* something.

More petals shake loose from the pearlescent fabric as her movements become sharper, more frantic, matching the shrill and staccato notes. I'm too far away to be certain, but I think the streaks carving gashes in her painted mask are tears. This music is fearful. It's pained. It's the thrashing of a captured animal, tearing its own arm off in a desperate attempt to escape a fate worse than death.

My hands, clasped between my knees, twitch with the desire to lunge for her. To free her, or save her, or beg her to save *me*. The music swells, higher and tighter and shriller than ever before, and her body hunches, knees bending and shoulders curling in, like she's protecting her instrument from the onslaught. A mother hovering over her child. A lover providing cover in their final moments.

A few beats of silence later, she releases a shaky breath that echoes louder through the theatre than any note she's played. She doesn't stand, but her bow caresses the strings once more. This part of the movement is softer, kinder, gentler. It swaddles me, tending to the wounds inflicted by its predecessor. The warmth seems to seep into the body of the player too, loosening her movements and allowing her to slowly stand straight again. This time, her expression is relaxed. Or perhaps accepting. Like this compassion is the inevitable counterpoint to the violence she played.

I don't stymie the tears leaking from my eyes. She looks so content, so comforted. And I am *jealous*.

I envy the naivete it takes to believe that there is any natural counterbalance to brutality. I am a daughter of The Syndicate of Fate. Over the sixteen short years of my life, I have learned to *be* that violence, and to ensure there is no healing from it. I claw that hope of comfort away from those who don't deserve it, and I watch those who do be robbed of it anyway. The only true promise of peace in this world is death.

That is what I think about as the audience breaks into thunderous applause, and as she bows in another shower of golden petals, and as I take shadowed alleyways back to our villa. But as I climb up the stairs of the employee entrance, ditching my scarf in a fireplace along the way, I wonder if I'm wrong. Maybe there is a small amount of peace before death, a way for our minds to comfort ourselves before we enter oblivion.

I wonder if I died tonight, if I might see Alisa Zakharov in a halo of gold, and hear the soft notes of her strings beckoning me to the other side.

Chapter 1
Alice

I push the brim of my cap up to wipe my forehead of sweat, squinting hard against the blinding sun. The cold wind at the dock always tricks passengers into thinking they need to bundle up for our trips, but by the time we've been out on the water for an hour or so, they predictably strip their layers and seek out overpriced sodas and what little shade they can find.

"Anything off the starboard?" Captain Jimmy yells through the open window. As usual, I'm parked on top of the roof of the cockpit, because it's as far up as I can get on this catamaran. The gritty metal and peeling paint dig into my skin through my cargo shorts, but I find it comforting.

"Nothing yet," I call back, tapping my tennis shoes against the window. The waters are too choppy to see spouts very clearly, but I'm hoping for birds. The birds never lie.

In my peripheral, I keep an eye on the customers, double-checking that no one is climbing the railings or running on the slick walk. Our first mate Allen is theoretically doing the same stern-side, but there's a good chance he's vaping in the bathroom instead.

We're a small crew of three and we bump heads often, but I can't complain. I get to spend nearly every day on the water, free of walls, cameras, and watchful eyes. Free of expectations, and of that nothingness that filled my every waking moment until five years ago. And Jimmy pays me under the table, which means I can continue operating without a bank account—and any verifiable identity.

After a lifetime of being told exactly who I am and will be, I am thrilled to be no one.

I'm lifting my water bottle to my lips when a movement to the north catches my eye. A flash of blue against blue, invisible to anyone who doesn't know what they're looking for. I push my binoculars up under my sunglasses and hold my breath while I scan the area. Waiting.

There it is again. Just a flash, but it's there.

"Jimmy, four o' clock," I yell, stomping on the glass to get his attention. I can't see him, but I feel the ship's engine rev a little. "Two of them, I think."

Jimmy doesn't move until he sees it too, but it only takes the tip of a fin breaking the surface of the ocean for him to thrust the boat into high gear. I grip the thin railing with one hand as I flick on the microphone that was tucked in my pocket.

"Alright, everyone, hang on to the railing! We're picking up speed to see if we can catch some friends waving to us in the distance!" My tone is like sugar and bubbles, as I've learned Americans like in their tour guides. They prefer overt sweetness and impossible enthusiasm in their service workers. I've watched about a thousand YouTube videos to perfect the effect.

Footsteps clamber as patrons who were hiding from the sun emerge from the cabin to get a glimpse at the very thing they paid forty-eight dollars a head to see. This trip is busier than most, and parents hoist their children up so they can see over the heads of adults leaning over the railing. We come to a slow stop, dipping and climbing with the rough waves as we all silently scan the surface.

"Starboard!" Allen's voice rings out from inside the cockpit. No idea when he got there, but I shuffle to the right and watch the long, gliding spine of a blue whale dip beneath the surface.

"Okay, everybody, we've got a few blue whales! Head to the starboard side of the boat. That's your right-hand side, if you're facing the front," I remind the passengers as they scurry around the railing. "Bottom or top level is totally fine, and remember to stay near the back if you're feeling seasick."

There are definitely seasick passengers today. Many of them. Most of whom refuse to believe that it's *much* worse to be sick inside a tiny, hot, enclosed bathroom than it is to hurl off the stern, no matter how much I promise them that's the truth.

A second blue whale arches from the water, a spout of mist emerging from its blowhole as its pockmarked back glides easily through the choppy waves. We get a tiny peek at her dorsal fin before she begins her dive, her fluke flattening against the water to propel her into the great deep.

"Look at how wide her tail is! Whale tails are called *flukes*, and they're incredibly strong. These kinds of whales can dive over a thousand feet."

There are murmurs of appreciation and wonder, which make the corners of my lips twitch with a smile. I love to watch people, especially kids, learn about these awe-inspiring creatures for the first time. It reminds me of sitting in my bed, a picture book splayed open in my lap, as my mother explained to me the different habitats of the sea.

A boy about six years old, with tight curls and a bright smile, turns to me from his perch atop his father's shoulders.

"Is a T-Rex bigger than a whale?" He asks like he's sure of the answer. Because to a six-year-old, nothing has ever been bigger than a dinosaur.

"There are some small whales, but blue whales like this one are the biggest animals to ever live on the whole planet," I say into the microphone, grinning at the way the kid's jaw drops open. "Actually, a blue whale weighs as much as thirty T-Rexes."

"No freaking way!"

The crowd laughs at his exclamation, and the child's dad shoots me a thankful grin as they turn back to watch the water. We follow the path the whales are travelling, a safe distance behind, as we watch their trips to the surface.

I spout off more blue whale facts, my voice grainy as it booms from the outdated speaker system. We're lucky enough to see a true dive, where the smaller of the pair lifts their fluke completely out of the water to a chorus of cheers.

By the time we're heading back to shore, the boat is buzzing. Even the passengers who have been sick most of the trip can muster a grimace, probably thankful we're almost back on dry land. I walk around the crowd with a dry husk of baleen in my hands, teaching the crowd about different types of whale teeth and feeding patterns. Allen grabs me by the elbow when we enter the harbor, and I help secure *La Ballena* to the tie-off. Patrons make their way off the catamaran on shaky legs, grasping soda cans and thanking me. The kid who asked about the dinosaurs even gives me a high-five, which is adorable.

I stretch under the heat of the sun, slipping off my cap and teasing my hair at the roots, trying to dry the sweat that's stuck it to my forehead. I'm standing on the edge of the gangplank, the toes of my sneakers teetering at the edge between the sea and the shore.

"Alice! It's your turn to clean the head."

I breathe out steadily, grateful for a reason to stay on the water a little while longer. Even a reason as disgusting as this one.

The familiar scrubbing, tidying, and logging associated with returning to shore is soothing. I draw it out as long as possible, even though both Allen and Jimmy try to move me along quicker. But the moment I step off this ship, I'll have to think about what snakes and spies lie on land.

Finally, I can't avoid the end of this shift any longer. I begrudgingly disembark, and Jimmy hands me an envelope of cash as we lock up, which I stuff in my back pocket as we make our way to the parking lot. I don't own a car—it seemed like an unnecessary risk, with no license and no insurance—so I head toward my bike, chained to the gas meter behind our ticket booth, as my crewmates grunt their goodbyes and head the other direction.

I can't help the anxiety that snakes through my veins every moment I'm not hidden on *La Ballena*. I've prepared for what comes next, but I know there's an invisible target on me, a scope aimed at my heart, that makes me sprint to the little locked shed from which we sell tickets.

My escape is hindered by a woman staring at our pricing sign. She's tall—at least half a foot taller than me—with light brown skin and straight, dark hair that skims her shoulders. She readjusts her backpack as she squints at the display behind dirty plexiglass, and the movement drags the collar of her top far enough that the tattooed wing of a bird peeks out from beneath the fabric.

"Can I help you with something?" I ask as I get closer, cursing myself for not hiding behind the shed until she leaves. There are some habits that are harder to break than others, and the need to offer help, to be amenable and pleasant at all times, is one of mine.

She turns toward me, and suddenly I have more empathy for the seasick passengers on my cruise. Her smile is bright and sharp, and the sight of it makes my stomach drop unpleasantly.

"Hi there," she says, lifting her sunglasses and pushing them into her hair. Her eyes drag up and down my body like she's performing an assessment. "You work here?"

She's pointing at the ticket booth, and I know I should answer, but it takes a moment to make my brain function properly. I've experienced attraction before, but it's always been closely coupled with shame. As a girl, my peers would whisper and giggle about the kids in town they had crushes on, and I so desperately wanted to join them and feel that camaraderie. But it was too ingrained in me that attraction was unseemly for a girl of my position. I knew from a young age that my parents would choose a match for me when I was older, and any fleeting relationships between now and then would be fleeting and potentially embarrass my father. Crushes and childhood sweethearts would only make the inevitable arranged, political partnership I was destined for more difficult, I was told.

So I drowned those instincts. And each time they've bubbled up since I've left Russia, they've been accompanied by guilt and nausea, followed by regret that I can't seem to strip those responses from my memory as easily as I have my accent and taste in music.

And none of these feelings are the fault or responsibility of the striking, slightly intimidating woman asking about my job.

"Yes," I stutter, fishing my keys off my carabiner and unlocking the rolling window cover. "Did you need to buy tickets?"

She smiles wider at me, and I hide my blush by hustling behind the counter, shaking the computer awake. She taps her fingernails against the smooth wooden counter, drumming like she has to think about my question.

"No, but I thought someone who worked here might be able to help me," she says, and when I force myself to look at her, her expression is pleading and a little guilty. "I'm here on a research grant to study the changing habitat of the Black Sea Nettle, but the service my program contracted to take me out on the water flaked. Do you know anyone who could help?"

I tried to school my features, hiding my surprise as she lays a photocopied nautical map on the counter. There are a few zones in the open ocean marked in faded yellow highlighter.

"Um..." I hesitate, staring at her sheet to avoid eye contact. "I guess it depends. When and how often are you going out? Do you need equipment? Dive gear?"

Without preamble, the woman pulls a black folder out of nowhere and slides it across to me. When I look up in surprise, I find her rolling her bottom lip between her teeth, exposing a positively vampiric incisor that, for some reason, makes me feel my pulse in my fingertips.

"All the details are in there, and of course I'm open to negotiation since I'm in a pinch. And no dive equipment needed. I'm actually a little afraid of the ocean, to be honest. Definitely not dive certified."

Through the haze of whatever spell her perfume—actually, it might be cologne—has put over me, I feel my brow furrow.

"You're researching marine life and you're afraid of the ocean?" I ask, watching a brief blush dust over her cheeks.

She leans in closer to me, saying the words like they're a secret we share, or like she's teasing me. "I don't mind the shoreline, but the deep water? Spooky."

Her eyes are so pretty. Deep brown, with this hazy ring of gold around the edge. Sparkling like she knows the answers to all the silly questions I've ever asked myself.

I clear my throat and break her gaze, trying to fight the instincts beaten into me. *I'm allowed to recognize when people are attractive. I'm no longer promised like a prize to whoever my father says.*

"Well, the whale watching vessel is a Class III which is

probably too big, and it's usually booked all day during the summer," I hedge, glancing behind me at the lock box mounted on the wall. "But my captain has a Class II boat that he might be willing to rent out to you."

He'd be especially willing if she was willing to pay under the table. This whole town operates on non-reported income, which is one of the many reasons I felt so comfortable hiding here.

"I'd be willing to pay for a guide, too," she says, excitement making her voice a little higher. "I have some basic sailing experience, but it would be helpful to have someone with me who knows the area."

I can't seem to look up at her again, but I flip open the folder she handed over and scan the details absently, absorbing almost nothing. Jimmy will probably send Allen, since he's basically useless on the whale watching excursions. Poor girl.

"Okay, yeah, I'll ask my boss if he can spare anyone..."

"Thank you *so* much," she interrupts, putting her hands on top of mine, the touch like an electric shock. So few people touch me, other than the occasional handshake or high five after a trip, that it always short circuits my brain. "You have no idea how much you'd be saving my ass. Can I give you my number and you can text me or call me or whatever when your boss decides?"

I carefully slip my hands from beneath hers, needing the distance for my mouth to function again, and pull two faded business cards from the drawer next to the register.

"I don't have a cell phone, but I can call you from here tomorrow morning, or you can call in sometime after three. That's when we get back from our last whale-watching cruise," I say, flipping one of the cards over and handing her a pen. Her lips quirk at the corners slightly as she pulls the cap off with her teeth.

"No cell phone, huh? I'm really not in Kansas anymore," she mutters, scribbling her number on the cardstock.

"You study marine biology in Kansas?" I ask, bewildered. I'm not particularly familiar with the American midwest, but I'm pretty sure you can't get further away from the ocean than Kansas.

"What? No, that's not—" she shakes her head, laughing as she takes the second card with our phone number on the front. "It's a saying. Let me guess, you didn't grow up in the U.S.?"

My stomach clenches immediately, and I try to cover my fear with a laugh. I've perfected my accent, changed my style, and done *so* much research on American culture. But there will always be things I've missed, and those things might be what gets me fucking killed one day.

"Oh don't worry, me either," she reassures me, misreading my dread as embarrassment. "I was born in Italy, and I lived with my dad's family in Argentina for a few years. Didn't come to the States until college."

"Yeah, pretty new," I answer noncommittally, shrugging as I overanalyze the numbers she's scribbled down. "Anyway, I'll give you a call if I have an answer in the morning."

"Thanks again, really," she says, tapping the counter with her fingertips again before hiking her backpack further up on her shoulder and backing away. I slip the card with her phone number into my pocket, pressing my thumb into the edge.

"I'm sorry, I didn't ask your name," I call out as she turns toward the parking lot, making her do a full turn back toward me. It seems like she hesitates for a moment, but I can't see her expression clearly from this distance.

"Emily," she says, lifting her arm in an awkward little wave. "Emily Vargas."

Chapter 2
Emily

Even when I can't see her, I know she's beautiful.

I stand at the edge of the bluff, frigid wind whipping against my cheeks. Tendrils of hair that have slipped from their tie twist around my face. I'm drawn toward the ragged edge, even though the thought of the drop below paralyzes me. Bright yellow sunlight bleeds orange, red, and pink against the horizon, blending in the choppy waves of the ocean's surface. Among the whitecaps sits a catamaran, dipping and climbing with the movement of the water. And on its bow she stands.

I can't make out details, but seeing her yesterday has branded her image behind my eyelids. Short, petite, fragile. Like a flower, like a bomb. White-blonde hair pulled high into a ponytail, pale freckles that dance across her even-paler skin. Bright blue eyes, wide and framed by near-translucent lashes. The angles of her cheeks so severe they could cut the glass it seems like she's made of. She dances around the bow of the ship, a gaggle of passengers around her, pressing their bodies to the railing to look over the edge.

The thought of the depth of that water makes my stomach

churn, but I swallow hard against the sensation. I'm safe on land. Well, relatively safe. Still not a big fan of how far up I am.

I suck in a deep breath, trying to steady my heart rate. Alisa is a target. A mission. Nothing more, nothing less. The girl I saw on stage all those years ago, bathed in warm light and wrapped in golden petals, is not the same one who presses herself against the ship's railing now. And I'm not the same person I was when I first saw her.

It was a lifetime ago, anyway. Before I had any real responsibility in The Syndicate. Before Alisa's father was more than a mid-tier longshoreman with a penchant for making connections and looking the other way. More than a decade has passed since I watched this girl pull a horsehair bow across viola strings in front of a crowd.

I force myself not to be enraptured by the memory. I was just a teenager with a crush, obsessed with the prettiest girl I'd ever seen in the way most teenagers are. I'm no longer the rebellious, carefree girl who went back to that theatre four times in a week, to watch the girl who shone like gold play over and over again.

She doesn't even use the same name. Alisa Zakharov is a ghost, neither dead nor alive. Schrodinger's victim. Alice Zimmerman is the shadow I've been hunting for the past six weeks. And Alice is who I have to extract information from before Clara, Charlie, and Bea decide to do it the old fashioned way.

I repack my equipment into my bag, trying to be careful with the camera Deniz let me borrow. I'm not much of a surveillance expert but he definitely is, and the gear he set me up with me is professional-grade. I try very hard not to think about the fact that he used this exact equipment to infiltrate my own family, via Clara.

Man, this family really needs to address how often we stalk the people we end up romantically involved with.

I'm both reluctant and relieved to leave my perch on this cliff, peeking over my shoulder a few times to watch the little speck of a catamaran on the water as I huff it back to my car. Alice didn't call me this morning, so I took the opportunity to watch her from afar, to try to gather information on her daily routine.

If she's working for her father, I can't imagine what utility she is to him here. Despite it being Nesika Beach's purported *busy season*, it's fairly dead. There are two motels on the main drive along the ocean, and both of them have plenty of vacancies. The patrons who sail on Alisa's—I mean *Alice's*—whale watching excursions are far more likely to trek the extra half hour south to Brookings or north to Port Oxford, towns with chain restaurants and corporate hotel options. And I really don't blame them.

Bea's voice rings in the back of my mind, reminding me that Alice doesn't have to be working for her father to be *of use* to us. If she really did fake her death all those years ago, she is an objectively invaluable bargaining chip to get Konstantin where we want him.

As far as I know, no one in my family knows about that night in Vladivostok. Obviously Zia Lucia's trip wasn't a secret, and neither was my accompanying her, but Alisa only made one formal appearance, strung on her father's arm like an accessory, albeit an angelic one. She hadn't spoken to a single soul, only floated around the room in Konstantin's shadow, disappearing before Lucia and I had even been introduced.

No one knows about my midnight treks to that wine bar. Or the way the girl painted in a sunrise bouquet became the standard of beauty I've held everyone else to from that moment on.

I know I'm biased, that I can't be objective in my assessment of her. But I couldn't allow my cousins to kidnap and torture her, not without at least trying to prove she knows nothing. What comes after that...I'm not ready to contemplate.

I drive back into town, if you could even call it that. There's two bars, both equally dive-y. A church with a moth-eaten couch on the lawn. A diner, a pawn shop, a liquor shop, and a discount store. There are a few houses tucked back off the main road, along with some mobile homes and one run-down apartment complex, which Alice lives in.

Upon initial assessment, the only building I found in the entire town with a security camera was the liquor store, which Deniz was easily able to access. The feed is dull, but I still click the disguised app on my phone that Clara's fiancé set up, watching the thirty-something owner stare at the TV on the counter.

All the other cameras in town are ones I've placed.

As I drive down Nesika Road, the few locals milling about crane their necks to stare. It's not often that a new face stays more than a day or so, and I've made my intentions to be around for the next few months rather obvious. On a normal mission I'd lay low, try not to draw attention to myself, but there's little point here. Every small change is the talk of the town.

Luckily, as far as Deniz and I can tell, we haven't drawn the attention of anyone outside the eight mile radius of this town, which we can only pray holds. The last thing we need is for Konstantin to catch wind that we're hunting his daughter. Unfortunately, the children of The Syndicate are much less subtle than Alice has been.

When I pull into the otherwise-empty motel lot, the owner makes a show of leaning against the open door to the tiny lobby. A lit cigarette hangs from her fingers—a Marlboro red, if I'm recalling the scent correctly—as she watches me unload my backseat. I wave a little too enthusiastically at her, which only makes her glare harder. If I was anyone else, the lack of trust might sting, but these people *shouldn't* trust me.

Plus, it probably doesn't help that I told her I don't want housekeeping service while I'm here. I'm sure she assumes I'm doing something highly illegal in her establishment, but I paid well over the market rate in cash in advance for my entire planned stay. Money buys a lot of things.

Once inside my dingy room, the exhaustion of the last few days finally hits me. This is part of the reason I hate surveillance, and prefer non-human research. I don't have to put on an act or consider my positionality when I'm analyzing data or trekking through the forest to find some lethally poisonous frog. And while my preference for solitude has put me in some sticky situations in the past—Clara will never forget the time I nearly died in a swamp because I insisted I could handle venomous snakes without a safety buddy—I sometimes think I'd rather die of hubris than deal with this many people.

I force myself to lock my equipment in the stormcase I shoved in the closet before flopping down on the least comfortable mattress I've ever been on. I've slept on train floors and the beds of pickup trucks, but the moment I pulled up the review photos of this place, I bought bed bug spray and a mattress protector.

You can do this. Your family is everything to you. Your mother and aunts have carried an empire on their shoulders to make the world a better place. That is your legacy. Alisa is no one.

I've repeated a variation of that mantra to myself over and over the past six weeks I've been preparing for this mission. And for the most part, it's soothed me. It's normal to form attachments, especially at such a young age, when I was only beginning to fully understand my sexuality. So I kept tabs on Alisa over the years, including her in any research about Konstanin as an excuse to see her face on surveillance tapes. And sure, I may have been surprised by how affected I was by her engagement to one of the Andreeva brothers, and by how gutted I was at the news of her death.

But she was a figment of my fantasies. An ethereal girl I cast in resin and held to the light when I needed to remind myself I could feel things. That the emotions she stirred within me as she played her music hadn't been drowned by the blood on my hands.

But she was *only* that. An object. A tool. And that should make it even easier to do what I must. I need to figure out how to objectify her in a new way. Use her to prove something much more important than my own humanity.

The water stain on the popcorn ceiling stares back at me. Doesn't feel like a great omen.

I slip my phone out of my pocket and hold it above my face, squinting at the screen as I read through Clara's messages. As always, she's made her lists. Objectives, timelines, requirements for updates. She knows something's up, and she's keeping a stricter watch over my work than she ever has before. Honestly, I'm surprised she agreed to let me come here in the first place; my argument wasn't that strong. It could be Deniz. I wouldn't say he's made her soft—the opposite, in fact—but he's certainly made her more curious.

Maybe she's just as tired of all the death as I am.

My other phone buzzes in my pocket—the burner I purchased specifically to communicate with Alice—and it shakes me out of my contemplation. There's no point in meditating on Clara's thought process. It's not like she's ever going to share it with me anyway.

The burner's screen flashes a familiar number, and I feel

my pulse pick up a step. *The adrenaline of the mission,* I convince myself as I pick up.

"This is Emily," I answer brightly, layering on the sunshine-y researcher persona I've donned for this mission.

"Um, hi. This is Alice. From the boat thing. That you needed."

She sounds anxious, but not fearful. Like she doesn't talk to people one-on-one much. Or maybe she doesn't talk on the phone often. She wasn't lying, she doesn't own a cell phone. I checked.

"Alice, great to hear from you," I say, putting the phone on speaker as I roll onto my stomach. "I hope you have good news for me."

She hesitates on the other end of the line, and there's a brief moment where I wonder if I've miscalculated Jimmy's need for untraceable income. The interest on his two boats is criminal, and he's swimming in online sports betting debt. I assumed leaving a copy of the fake contract with my fake previous charter with a fake, yet laughably large, service fee would be all the convincing he needed.

"Yes, well, sort of," she finally stumbles, and I hear her tap a keyboard, what seems like a nervous habit. "He can agree to three days per week, six hours per day, on the Class II. But the payment will have to be cash only, due to some..." Alice pauses again. "Banking issues."

Banking issues. More like *I don't want the government garnishing this for my vessel registration fees.*

"That's not a problem," I promise lightly, thinking about the absolutely criminal stack of bills tucked into the stormcase. "The university provided me with a research stipend, I'm sure it'll cover it."

"Oh," she replies simply, the surprise evident in her voice. "Okay, that's good then. You can leave the payment with me at the ticket stand tomorrow, before you go out. He said he can spare the boat Tuesdays through Thursdays."

"Works perfectly for me," I say, thrilled that this worked out as smoothly as it did, and suspicious that this may be the last thing that goes so well this entire trip.

"Okay, well..."

"Did he say anything about a guide?" I cut her off before she can hang up on me. This was the part I had the least control over. I have contingency plans if Jimmy offers up Allen, but I'd rather not employ them. Allen seems like a good kid, despite being addicted to blue-raspberry-flavored THC vapes and his questionable internet search history. He takes care of his grand-father. He sends his little cousins knockoff Lego sets. I really don't want to give him a gastrointestinal virus that will haunt his nightmares for the rest of his life.

"Right, yeah, I'll be helping you." Victory. The simple, sweet feelings of luck and circumstance being on your side.

"Wonderful," I reply, not having to feign positivity in the slightest. "What time should I meet you?"

Alice and I make our arrangements, and she's quick to get off the phone after we've confirmed the basics, but nothing can puncture the little bubble of triumph in my chest. The exhaustion that weighed on me when I first laid down has disappeared, and a familiar euphoria-driven adrenaline pumps through my veins, making my legs bounce.

This is who I am. Winning, achieving, learning—those things are what make me feel like this. A new personal record on my deadlift. Finding the corrupt code in a data file and watching the information flow perfectly. Getting a perfect culture swab on the first try. Seeing the fight leave your victim's eyes when you've pushed them to their breaking point.

The sensation fills my veins like champagne, and I quickly strip and change into workout gear, needing to burn off the energy pumping through me. I double check the locks on the stormcase, confirm all Deniz's surveillance cameras are still monitoring for any motion in this room, and slip my earbuds in.

The air is thick and chilly in my lungs, but I keep running. Out of the motel lot, down the main road, over hiking trails, off beaten paths. It takes hours of searing lungs, thumping music, and heavy breaths before the adrenaline subsides, and I'm clear-headed enough to plan what to do with my target tomorrow.

Chapter 3
Alice

The wind tangles my hair as we make our way out to open ocean. It's overcast, like it is most mornings, haze blotting out the horizon. It comforts me like a blanket. Out here in the middle of the water, with such little visibility, I'm no one. No target on my back, no fear of who I'll see on the street, no scheming—finally the ghost I've always wished I could be.

Emily, it seems, is not comforted by the fog. That, or her fear of the ocean is more serious that I realized. For all that charm and all those muscles, she isn't as brave as I imagined she would be. She's clearly trying to exude confidence, with her arm stretched out over the back of the cushioned-lined seats and her ankle crossed over her knee, but her white-knuckled grip on the railing gives her away.

She was chatty when she first turned up at the ticket booth, laden with a backpack and two heavy-looking black waterproof cases. But the closer we got to the dock, the more her smile seemed forced, and her answers to my logistical questions became shorter and more clipped.

I'm taking it slow for her sake, but it still only takes us a little over an hour and a half to get to the starting coordinates she provided me. It's been a silent trip, and I'm pretty sure Emily's keeping her mouth shut so she doesn't puke.

"We're here," I say, killing the engine. The sudden silence makes Emily blanch, which I guess I can understand. Surrounded by mist, without the distraction of a machine pushing you along, you can feel very vulnerable out here.

Or so I'm told.

"Right, do you need to drop an anchor or something?" she asks, still gripping the railing tightly. She hasn't moved a muscle.

"This anchor chain is about thirty-five feet," I say, less gently than I probably should to someone who looks like they're barely suppressing a panic attack. Emily swallows hard, donning a very wobbly smile.

"I assume the ocean is quite a bit deeper here."

"Aren't you a professional marine biologist?"

She laughs, a too-loud cough that seems to shake her of some of her nerves. She lets go of the railing and scrubs her face before shaking out her hands.

"Actually, I'm a toxicologist," she says, almost like it's a joke. "I specialize in cnidarians. Corals, jellies, anemones, stinging things. But most of my work so far has been in a lab. Field work is new to me."

Something about her explanation feels...off. Sure, she seems afraid of the ocean itself, but she handles the equipment with ease. She fiddled with a lot of the gadgets as I prepared the boat, and she seemed pretty familiar with them to me.

I'm about to press, but I stop myself. There's no point. She doesn't owe me honesty, and I'm certainly not going to be able to provide it in kind. I'm the last person to judge someone for half-truths and omissions.

"A few nautical miles offshore, we hit the continental slope.

It goes down almost three thousand feet, though we're not at the deepest part."

Emily breathes in deeply through her nose, that slightly crazed smile locked on to her face.

"That makes sense. Black Sea Nettles live all along the ocean column, but they like cold water because of the abundant food. In Baja they're found closer to the surface, but here...well, that's what I'm here to research, right?"

I really don't know what she's here to research, but I nod, and she seems to take that as encouragement. She starts unloading equipment—sampling bottles, very fancy looking cameras, things I couldn't identify with a gun to my head. She lifts what looks like a drone out of the larger case. It has a long, umbilical cord-like tether attached, and she works like it's muscle memory to set everything up.

Not familiar with field research. Sure.

I don't ask any more questions. I shouldn't have asked any to begin with. I know they're almost always returned, and I can never respond honestly. But it feels so easy out here, in the heart of the sea. No one can hear the words you whisper. No one could even hear you scream. The thought should be terrifying, especially with a stranger who is clearly physically stronger than me. Instead, like everything the ocean offers, it puts me at ease.

I sip from my water bottle, listen to the waves roll against the hull, watch the GPS to ensure we don't drift too far from Emily's coordinates. She hums to herself. Turns things on and off and back on again. Checks and rechecks her equipment.

The sun rises a bit more, and the haze slowly starts to burn off. In the distance, I spot the spout of a whale. My fingers twitch instinctually to move toward it, but I grin at the little puff of smoke dissipating into the air.

"I'm going to drop the ROV now."

Emily's voice is like lightning in a rainstorm, and I startle enough that I drop my metal water bottle, which thunks so loudly it makes Emily trip over herself. We're both apologizing, talking over each other as we lean to grab the bottle.

"Sorry, didn't mean to..." she starts, getting to the dented bottle first and holding it out to me.

"No, I dropped—" I reply, avoiding her gaze as I snag it from her, accidentally brushing over her hand as I do. We both apologize again, and I grip my beloved water bottle even tighter to stymie the tingling feeling in my fingertips where my skin touched hers.

Excitement and guilt tangle themselves up in my chest again, and I shove the nausea-inducing feeling deep down. Not because I'm ashamed of my attraction to her this time—she's objectively gorgeous, and I'm a human being with eyes—but because we're both working. And from what I can tell, we're both lying to each other. And to top it all off, I'm putting her at risk by letting her be this close in proximity to me for so long.

It's complicated.

After a few beats of silence, Emily gestures to the little robot balancing on the edge of the railing.

"I'm going to drop the ROV into the water, and then I'll have to optimize the depth and confirm the settings. Then I can monitor the feed for the rest of the time," she explains slowly, like she's trying not to spook me.

"So you just watch that screen?" I ask, looking at the tablet-like device she's set up on one of the bench cushions. "You don't have to do anything else?"

"Well, I'll collect some water samples. And if we had any jellies come up close to the surface, I could theoretically place an acoustic tag, but I doubt we'll be that lucky," she explains, hovering her hands over equipment and resources as she talks. "But yeah, it's mostly watching and recording."

So hours of sitting here, staring at a six inch screen in silence. Perfect.

I lean back in my chair and watch as she unwraps the umbilical cord thing from its reel, glancing over her shoulder at the monitor again and again. When she's satisfied with the slack, she grips the robot gingerly and leans over the railing, placing it gently on the surface of the water. I stretch so I can observe as the little thing bobs in the gentle waves, tipping side to side before small oxygen bubbles create a skirt around it, and it begins to sink beneath the surface.

And then there's nothing. The cord slips further over the edge, and it takes a very long time before it is taut. The monitor flickers in strange shades of green and blue. The boat sways, the haze lifts, the birds call.

And Emily sits across from me, staring at her screen.

At least the silence is peaceful. And while still gorgeous, Emily is significantly less intimidating now that I know she's terrified of the sea. Who could be fearful of something so limitless? Sure, it's natural to be wary of the unknown, but I'll never understand how others aren't calmed by the knowledge that we're nothing more than a speck of dust in comparison to the vastness of the ocean.

"So, how'd you get into boats?"

When I turn to her, Emily isn't looking at me, and I wonder if I hallucinated her question. After a few beats of silence though, she glances up from her screen, eyebrows raised.

"Me?" I ask, fiddling with the mouth of my water bottle.

"No, the ROV," she scoffs, leaning over to the control panel to adjust something. "Yes, you."

"Right. Um..." I stutter, rolling my neck out and I decide how much of the truth to tell her. Lies are easier to keep the more reality you imbue them with. "My mom loved the ocean. She used to take me out to sit on the docks and tell me stories about mermaids and pirates. Said I should learn to sail, because she never got to."

That's about ninety-nine percent true. She never told me to learn to sail. She knew better than to inspire me to dream of things I couldn't have.

"That's cute," Emily says, glancing over the edge of the railing and balancing. "No offense, but I can't imagine enjoying this."

I bristle a little, but try to brush it off. People don't need to love things as much as I do. Not even the people who are *paid* to research the things I love.

"I understand why some don't like it. The vastness can be intimidating," I admit, though I can't keep the sliver of wonder from my voice. " But that's really what makes me love the sea. The mystery, the endlessness, the knowledge that you're only a tiny, unimportant organism in the marine web of life, floating like the rest of it."

"Really comforting, thanks," Emily grumbles, sounding less congenial than before. "You could work on your bedside manner."

"I was trying to commiserate," I huff, annoyed at her change in attitude. I get that she's afraid, but she doesn't need to be so pushy about it. "And also, I'm not your nurse, I'm your chauffeur."

"Are you always so combative?" she questions, her knees buckling as a particularly strong wave rolls us. I barely have to shift my weight.

"Are you always this much of an ass to the people you hire?"

She whips her head back at me, shock that almost looks like betrayal on her face. It takes her a moment, but she soothes her features, looking down at her shoes and breathing deeply.

"Sorry, caged animal syndrome, you know?" she explains. I

get it, I really do. I'm familiar with the urge to bite back with venom when things attack. But it's not me that she's afraid of, and I'm certainly not the reason she's here.

I could continue to be pissed, but it's not worth the effort. I twist in my seat, readjusting my posture to relieve the pressure in my back.

"Have you always been afraid of the ocean?" I want to make a joke to cut the tension, ask her if she almost drowned or **морской змей** nibbled on her fingers as a kid, but she doesn't seem like she's in the joking mood. And I can't remember the English word for **морской окунь**.

"It's more the fear of the unknown. Or not being in control." Perhaps subconsciously, she adjusts one of the settings on the monitor. Something she *can* control. "Humans have explored approximately one percent of the ocean, so we have no idea what's lurking beneath us. Storms can come out of nowhere. Boat engines can stop functioning correctly. And we're out here alone, with very few resources."

"With that mentality, you'd have to be afraid of airplanes. And eating at restaurants. Actually, you'd have to be afraid of pretty much everything..."

Emily is staring purposefully at the screen, like she can will away my conclusion by sheer force. I think she's biting the inside of her cheek.

"Are you really? Afraid of everything?" The concept is foreign to me. Sure, I'm afraid of *some* things. I truly hate snakes. And obviously I fear my father and Ilya, and what they will do when they find me. But to fear anything I don't have complete control over?

"It's complicated," she mutters, unwilling to look directly at me. "And obviously I face the fears. I'm here, aren't I?"

"Yes, but constantly combating your fight or flight instinct has to be exhausting," I say, for the first time feeling bad for the woman across from me.

"It makes me stronger," she says, mostly to herself.

"Survival doesn't make you stronger, it just makes you survive," I argue, mostly to *myself*. "You work out, right? Muscles need rest and care to heal and grow. If you keep working them to exhaustion, eventually they'll fail."

Emily looks at me like I slapped her across the face. Something flits across the screen, but it's not a jellyfish.

"Not everyone has the luxury of avoiding what they're afraid of," she bites out, something like resentment flickering across her face. I nearly choke suppressing a laugh. Yes, a life of hiding from Ilya and my father has been nothing short of opulent.

"Who said you should run from them?" I argue, my eyes catching on another spout in the distance. "There are differences between avoiding your fears, facing them, and overcoming them."

Emily's incredulous expression doesn't change, like my words don't have any meaning to her. If I hadn't had to search for the English word *overcoming*, I would have thought I accidentally slipped back into Russian.

I don't say anything else, and neither does she. For the next three hours we watch the monitor in silence, not a single sea nettle to be found. Eventually, she looks down at her watch, and without explanation starts reeling in her ROV and packing up her materials. I put the boat in gear and let the roar of the engine fill the silence thick between us.

And when I'm roping the boat to the bollards, I remember the word I was looking for. **морской змей**. Sea snake.

Chapter 4
Emily

"I thought you were supposed to be researching rockfish."

My laptop is propped open on my bed, and the hotel room is small enough that I can hear Charlie's voice from the bathroom where I'm brushing my teeth.

"My PhD advisor suggested the topic change to coincide with a climate change grant," I yell through a mouth full of toothpaste. Charlie grumbles about how he *can't understand a word I'm saying* as I spit into the sink and splash water on my face.

"Didn't we give them the money for the research? Don't we decide what you study?" Clara mutters irritably. I can tell she's distracted because usually she would be much more bitchy about something like this.

"The donation was anonymous. And it would be pretty suspicious if I insisted on arguing with my advisor about the species of venomous animal we should spend weeks hunting down when I'm supposed to be worshipping the ground she walks on," I shout into the main room while tugging on my cargo pants. "Plus, why do you care? We did the important part

—we found the city Alisa was in and made up a reason to be here."

To be fair, I was a little disappointed that I wasn't going to be able to stick with the rockfish cover. Mostly because they hang out in more shallow waters than these fucking jellies.

"As long as you're getting information out of her, you can get stung or bit by whatever you want," Clara says. I'm fully dressed and decent, so I move back in front of the laptop so I can see them. Gwen is on her first solo mission for The Syndicate—I think Clara sent her just to see Charlie squirm—and Bea's phone went straight to voicemail when we started the call, so it's only Clara, Deniz, and Charlie on the screen.

"It's been a day and a half. Let me warm up a little," I say, trying to infuse my normal irreverent charm to hide whatever inexplicable emotion is stuck in my chest.

My first day with Alice was not at all what I expected. She was...argumentative. Almost combative. Despite over a decade of keeping tabs on her from a distance, I never expected her to be anything but docile. Particularly knowing Konstantin would never have tolerated a hostile daughter. But the realization shook me for a reason I couldn't pinpoint until late into the night.

It took hours of laying in this bed and staring at the ceiling to accept that I had *objectified* Alisa. All these years, I had taken the few moments I actually spent in her vicinity and built an imaginary person on them. I know a lot of things *about* her— her blood type, the languages she speaks, the way she prefers her coffee—but I don't *know* her.

It makes the work I have to do so much easier. She's not this shimmering standard of beauty that I've been mooning over since I was a teenager. Like Clara told me all those months ago, she's just a target.

So what if I've spent the last decade and a half watching

recordings of any event Alisa attended in the name of *research* to see her face again? Who cares if it felt like a gut punch when her engagement to the eldest Andreeva brother was announced? Or that I threw up in an airplane bathroom when I heard she died?

I was mourning the version of her I created in my head. Every time I thought of Alisa over the past decade, I imagined the girl on stage, the quiet and creative excellence, the sly smile she would give her father at events, the gentle and delicate way she laughed when paraded around by Ilya. I mourned *Alisa*, whoever I thought she was.

But Alice? She's nothing to me. A puzzle I have to solve to get one step closer to destroying Konstantin and avenging the attack on Lucia. Separating the childhood crush from the woman before me is necessary, for the success of my mission and for my own sanity.

I am a daughter of The Syndicate of Fate. I know better than anyone that the means will eventually be justified by the ends. Alice may be a victim of her fathers villainy, but so is Lucia. And my allegiance is to the family who has loved and protected and mentored me my whole life, not the girl I had a childhood crush on.

If I have to sacrifice her to her father, so be it.

"Emily, are you listening to me?"

Clara's voice is no longer distracted. I shake myself out of the spiral I was falling down and focus on the screen, displaying her very pissed face.

"Sorry, no I wasn't," I admit, turning around to load my backpack with the equipment I charged last night. "Was thinking through my plan for the day."

"Well I suggest you get your act together, because if you don't confirm beyond a shadow of a doubt that she's not involved with her father, *and* milk every ounce of information you can about his operations out of her, by the end of August, we will."

I whip around before I can control the expression on my face, the solar charger for ROV slipping from my fingers and landing with a thud on the dirty carpet. I've known Clara my entire life, so the carefully controlled and commanding expression on her face is easy to read. She's pushing me because she knows something is up. She has since the moment we realized Alisa was alive. It's her job to pry and pick at the weaknesses in our ranks, not only to ensure the mole that betrayed her mother is unearthed and exterminated, but to safeguard the future of The Syndicate.

It's her job to question me, to make me prove my undying loyalty to The Syndicate and our family. Even if she loves me. *Especially* because she loves me.

"I was under the impression I had until the end of the year," I say carefully, knowing an outright argument would get me nowhere. It's only family on this call, so we get some leeway, but even here I can't go so far as to openly defy an order or question her leadership.

"Circumstances have changed," she replies in monotone, not a shred of emotion in her voice. "Ilya returned to Russia for a few weeks when Konstantin's men found what we left of his brother, but he's back now. Outside of Sacramento this time."

My stomach dips, fear crawling through my veins as I curse under my breath. We really hoped our handling of Lev—the obvious torture, the burned remains, the indignity with which we left his charred bones on Konstantin's proverbial doorstep— would make them hesitate to take more action. But I should have known that Konstantin would be willing to sacrifice anyone to get his daughter back under this thumb.

"Do we think he knows where she is?" I ask, not certain if

I'm afraid of the answer or looking forward to it. I can handle Ilya Andreeva on my own. He fights dirty, but I'm worse.

It's keeping Alice alive in the crossfire that concerns me. If I'm going to sacrifice my first love, I'm certainly going to get more out of her than an Andreeva. We need Konstantin.

"We're monitoring his movements as best we can, but he's being more careful this time," Deniz replies. Clara's stone expression softens a little at the sound of his voice. "He's not going to be as hasty as his brother."

"Never was," Charlie mutters, dragging his tattooed hands through his hair. He's not wrong. The Andreeva brothers were known for their violence, but Ilya's was always more controlled, which made him far more dangerous.

"In any case, time is no longer our luxury. You get the information we need from her in the next six weeks, and figure out if she's worth enough to Konstantin to make himself vulnerable," Clara commands. Her edict hasn't changed since that weekend in the cabin, and I still haven't found a way around it.

"And if she's not, what's our plan? Abandon her here and let Ilya kill her? Or worse?"

Charlie keeps his gaze lowered, and Deniz is clearly staring at Clara through the screen. But my Matriarch doesn't flinch, doesn't shift a millimeter.

"Her life isn't our concern. If she's Konstantin's victim—and that's not yet certain—she has my sympathy. But I am not Bea, and I will not risk the safety of our family and our mission for the daughter of a monster." It's silent for a beat, and I think she'll end the meeting there. But something shifts—perhaps she meets her fiancé's eyes. "If you think she's worth saving...well, it seems you need a better plan."

"I FEEL like we got off on the wrong foot yesterday," I yell, hanging on to the railing of this horrifying boat for dear fucking life.

Alice doesn't turn around, which is fair. I don't think she can hear me over the wind and the roar of the engine. I'd get up and move closer to her if I wasn't half-convinced I'd be flung off this glorified dinghy into the sea.

The thought of the depths below me is harrowing. Dark, cold, unknown. Monsters and dangers who can see and smell your fear so acutely, you have no hope of hiding from or outrunning them. Floating in that open sea, with nothing around you for miles, is my version of hell.

Alice was eerily accurate when she said I'm afraid of everything. Fear plagues every moment of my existence. When I was young, it kept me from being the daughter of The Syndicate I was supposed to be. I didn't want to learn to swim, or wield a weapon, or even try new foods. Outside of well-controlled environments where I could dictate every variable and predict every potential outcome, I wanted nothing new.

Aunt Lucia blamed my parents. Said they were too soft on me, as the youngest. Though it was uncommon for the sitting Matriarch to take anyone under her wing except her successor, Lucia made an exception, teaching me to face my fears herself. Forcing me to defend myself against attacks. Throwing me into a lake and demanding I save myself.

Pitting Clara and I against each other, with our fists and our minds and our will.

It took me a long time to learn how to survive her, to survive my own panic. But now I know that no matter how afraid I am, it can't consume me. The panic lives in my chest like a snake, like a vise, constricting my heart and lungs every single second I'm forced to face a fear. And I survive it, because I am stronger and more cunning than that snake can ever be.

So I let it tighten in my chest. Like holding your fingertips to flame to dull the nerves, I allow that feeling slither into each bronchus of my lungs, suffocating me. I remind myself that it can't kill me. That I don't need to breathe. I just need to survive.

And once I've settled into that sensation, I force myself to stand. I slide my fingers across the railing as I walk toward Alice, tightening my grip at each bump and jolt, until I'm right next to her.

She smells like the sea. I think we could be a thousand miles from here and she'd still smell like salt and brine, sunshine and zinc. There are faded pink streaks in the white-blonde hair tucked under a baseball cap that I didn't notice yesterday, and I wonder when she decided to dye her hair.

"I said I think we got off on the wrong foot yesterday," I repeat, equally as loud. She still doesn't react, even though I know she heard me this time. "Look, I need you not to hate me so I can finish this research and get my PhD and graduate sometime in the next century. Please."

I wish this part was a lie, but it's painfully true. No amount of money or political influence or willingness to skin someone alive would convince the MIT Department of Biological Engineering that I deserved any amount of leniency or grace during the dissertation process. I love my work, and I appreciate how it benefits The Syndicate, but I would welcome a single molecule of understanding, emotional support, or recognition that I'm a human being and not a research robot from Dr. Devenigh, my advisor.

I think it's slightly more likely that Clara abdicates her throne and joins the circus.

Alice still doesn't respond to me, but her grip loosens on the wheel slightly, which I take as a positive sign. I keep my eyes firmly on the navigation equipment, pretending to be confused by it. Whoever said that keeping your eyes on the horizon makes you less seasick is a cruel liar. I'll be focusing on the things I can literally control for the foreseeable future.

We make it to our coordinates a lot faster today, probably because Alice is not taking it easy on me. As the boat slows, she rolls her shoulders and cracks her neck, steeling herself for the silence.

"Even if I hated you, I would still do this because I can't get fired from this job," she sighs, her eyes most *certainly* on the horizon. "But I was rude yesterday, so I should apologize. I'm stressed."

Despite the fact that she did *not* apologize, I shoot her a forgiving smile that she doesn't acknowledge.

"It's totally fine, I was unnecessarily standoffish. And same, stressed. About the research." I bump her shoulder with mine, which is a little difficult seeing how much shorter than me she is. "Truce?"

She finally looks at me, her chin tilted up and her eyes squinting against the bleak morning sun filtering through the haze. God, she's pretty. At least I didn't fabricate that.

"Truce."

It takes me less time to set up and adjust the equipment today, now that I'm used to the feeling that nearly freezes my cells as I lean over the edge to drop the ROV. The water is a little rougher today, and Alice has to turn the engine back on twice to adjust our position.

After the little robot has sunk to its appropriate depth—a job I am thankful belongs to machines and not me—I try to think through how to get Alice to open up to me. To let me crawl through her brain and pick all the pieces I need out like shards of glass from skin.

"So, how long have you been in Oregon?"

Her head whips up, her fingernails frozen under the sticker she was prying from her aluminum water bottle. Genuine terror flashes across her skin like lightning, disappearing as quickly as it came as she forces herself to relax.

"A few years," she says simply, locking in the customer service facade she had when we first met. Placid smile, serene attitude, like nothing can shake her.

I don't love that it makes me want to see how much she can take before she breaks.

"What made you choose this place?" I ask, writing down coded observations—both of the sea and of the woman across from me—in the spiral-bound jotter balanced on my knee.

"I was passing through town and saw they were hiring for the whale watching boat, and decided it was time for a change," she replies, the answer sounding clinically rehearsed. To anyone else, they would seem like the words of a woman who has been asked the same question by tourists a thousand times over.

"Staying here is certainly a *choice* though," I laugh, gesturing toward the shore like we can see the empty streets and abandoned buildings from here. "Were you from a small town before?"

She opens her mouth to respond and then freezes, the little smile she had nipping at the corner of her mouth dissipating. Back in place is that carefully empty, pleasant expression.

"You ask a lot of questions for a stranger," she says with a light laugh, her tone carefully curated to sound like the end of a conversation. But obviously that won't be happening.

"I'm a researcher, that's what I do," I wink, pretending I

don't get a little thrill from the blush that spreads along her cheeks. "And we're going to be out on this boat a lot together over the next few weeks. Would it kill us to get to know each other?"

She pulls her lower lip between her teeth, and for the first time it really is like I can read her mind. She must know that it *might* kill us to get to know each other. From her perspective, I could be a spy of her father's or her fiancé's, or simply a careless tourist who will open her mouth at an inconvenient moment and reveal her location to those hunting her. Talking to me, trusting me, is a risk.

But after a few moments of relative silence, save for the thump of the boat rocking in the waves and the gentle scrape of the ROV tether against the hull, she looks a little more resolute.

"I suppose we'll have to find out."

Chapter 5
Alice

I may have miscalculated my dose.

I'm hunched over the toilet for the third hour straight, completely nude and wishing I could shave my head so I didn't have to feel the strands stuck to my neck with sweat. My muscles spasm uncontrollably as my stomach clenches and I throw up more bile into the bowl, because there's nothing else left in me to expel.

Still, this isn't the worst post-ingestion reaction I've had. The first time I swallowed a vial of diluted rattlesnake venom, I honestly thought I had signed my own death certificate. I knew, getting into this whole mithridatism business, that accidental death was a possibility. Even likely. And while it would have been a shame to waste the efforts of all those who died to keep me alive, I still believe it's worth the risk.

Even if that belief is being tested at this moment.

My abdomen stops contracting, and I take the fleeting opportunity to lay back on the laminate floor, pretending it's cooling my overheated body. I've tried to convince myself I don't miss much about Vladivostok, about the prison that was my father's estate, but I can't even lie to myself that convincingly. I miss luxury. Marble floors, clean beds, soft linens, pretty dresses. At night I dream of thick rugs under my toes, and massive bathtubs filled with warm water and fragrant perfumes. I crave rich foods and fine wines, sparkling jewelry and experiences that only blood soaked money can buy.

And I'd leave it all over again.

The ocean breeze, cool and humid, filters through the long rectangular window over the shower, and eventually my body temperature starts to regulate. I know this isn't the end of the consequences of my misdosing—I've learned that rattlesnake venom poisoning is a long process to heal from, and I won't be truly out of the woods for at least two days—but I need to force myself to rest. I have another excruciatingly long day on that boat with Emily tomorrow, and I need to fortify myself with sleep.

I find my discarded sleepwear—a 3XL men's tee shirt with the words *Miami Beach Wet T-Shirt Contest Sponsor 1997* screen-printed on the back that I found at a thrift store outside Portland—and slip it back over my sweaty frame before climbing into bed. My flat is small, dark, and damp, the threadbare fold out couch and secondhand dresser my only real furniture. I stare, slightly delirious from dehydration and the effects of the venom, at the array of tchotchkes cluttering the top of my dresser. A humpback whale made out of chicken wire. A compact mirror gifted to me by one of the many roommates I've had as I floated around the Pacific Northwest. A notebook.

My mother's.

My vision fades in and out as I stare at that little green notebook. It was her favorite color. Seafoam green.

She loved the sea. She would sit and watch it all day. The East Sea. Not the Pacific Ocean, but close.

She would look at the same water I sail on. On the other side of the world.

The notebook is empty now. I had to. He couldn't find her words. But they live inside my mind. I memorized each and every one before I dropped the pages in the sea.

Sometimes I open it. I run my fingers over the first page. It has the indents...from what she wrote...her hand was there...

Fuᴄᴋ. I'm alive.

The alarm clock on the floor next to my overpriced pawn shop futon blares loudly. My head is pounding, and my mouth feels filled with cotton. Every single muscle in my body protests as I roll over and silence the alarm, screaming with the need to recuperate.

But unfortunately, I don't have that option.

In my state of the art kitchen, consisting of a sink, a mini fridge, a hot plate, and a microwave that saw the fall of the Berlin Wall, I make my customary breakfast of a microwaved burrito and water from the tap. It will have to tide me over until Emily and I get back to shore, because I've run out of anything appropriate to bring on the boat. Another trip to the discount store is necessary.

Before I get in the shower and steel myself for another day of Emily's questions, I slide open the bottom drawer of my dresser and fish the vials of venom out of the pocket of my only pair of jeans. They clink and clatter in my palm, the liquid viscous, yellow, and nauseating. I run my tongue over my teeth nervously as I shove the vials back in the pocket.

There's no point in washing my hair, it'll just get ruined as soon as we're on the boat, but I scrub myself and force myself to keep down my breakfast. I cannot throw up again. I will not survive this day if I have no food in my body.

Emily is inquisitive. Makes sense, being a researcher and all, but it's very new to me. My father never asked, he only demanded. He didn't inquire about my interests, because he believed he chose them for me. Ilya was similar, though less charismatic about it. He saw me for what I was—a tool to get closer to my father's empire. He never asked me questions, but his demands were less vocal. Never a spoken direction to stand here, talk to this person, go to my room, learn this piece on the piano, stop crying, don't talk about my mother. Rather, a hand, too harsh, on my lower back or around my elbow. A flicker in his eyes that I understood inherently as my cue to move or leave or smile.

Since my escape, I've kept to abandoned towns or massive cities, both venues where people leave you alone if you don't seem too friendly. In most towns, I've been able to pay cash to thrift and pawn shops, and provide vague answers and under the table rent to sketchy roommates.

Emily isn't like that. She wants to know everything, possibly everything *about everything*. She asks me about my childhood in the same tone that she used while muttering over the little robot's cord when the image on the monitor went out. Like the world is a book of things she hasn't read yet, about to be cracked open just for her.

I don't feel bad lying to her. She doesn't know me, doesn't care. She's as entertained by my half truths and fabricated stories as she would be by reality. And honestly, it's been surprisingly nice to give even the smallest parts of myself to someone. One day soon, when I'm dead or have become an irredeemable killer, a sliver of me will live on in the memory of this pretty genius who is afraid of the water she works on. There's some comfort in that, which I didn't expect.

When the shower runs cold, far too soon for my liking, I dry myself and slather a ridiculous amount of sunscreen onto my naked body, even the parts of me that will be covered by clothes. The sky may be overcast here most of the day, but the sun is sneaky, and I learned the hard way that my skin does not fare well in such conditions.

I wish that I could crawl back into bed and sleep off the effects of my misadventure last night, but I pull on my cleanest pair of shorts, a tee shirt, and a ball cap before grabbing the keys to Jimmy's boat. *At least it's not like the first time*, I remind myself. I've built up a good, if imperfect, tolerance by now. Eight months ago, a too-strong dose left me in bed for a week.

The bike ride to the dock isn't long, but it is peaceful, and it gives me the opportunity to think about the webs I'll spin for Emily today. I can be anyone with her. I can tell as much or as little of the truth as I want, and it means nothing out on the water.

The woman herself is standing at the mouth of the dock as I ride up, arms laden with her heavy gear as usual. I had offered to help her carry it off the boat yesterday when we returned to shore, but when I tried to lift the smallest of the cases, I realized I was out of my depth. If the muscles didn't give it away, her ability to carry all that equipment with a smile on her face certainly illuminated how strong she is.

I try not to stare at her smile as I lock my bike behind the ticket booth and make my way toward her. She's effortlessly pretty, in a way that's almost annoying. Somehow her strong body—lean and broad and tall—is perfectly complimented by her long eyelashes and swishy hair. I have to stop myself from trying to flick my salt-ridden ponytail over my shoulder in jealousy.

I have come to terms with the fact that she's attractive, that *I'm* attracted to her. But the acknowledgement still makes me feel guilty, like I'm cheating on the fiancé I never loved and faked my death to escape. Something inside still fears my father finding out I wanted something. Wanted *anything*.

He decided what was best for me. He knew the right dress, the right age to wear makeup, the right classes and languages and instruments, the right husband. Wanting was tantamount to treason in his eyes.

But wanting another *person?* Choosing love instead of creating it with the match he'd found for me? In my teenage years, I couldn't imagine a more significant way to betray my family.

But I suppose we're long past that. Faking your death and escaping to America trumps a Romeo and Juliet situation by a mile.

"Last day this week!" Emily exclaims cheerfully as she matches my stride toward the boat, her movements animated and jumpy. I suppose this is slightly better than the frozen fear from the last two days.

"I feel like you're overcompensating," I mutter, my voice cracking painfully with the memory of bile. I swallow hard against the feeling of microwaved eggs and cheese climbing up my throat.

"I am surviving," she replies with a little more bite, which almost makes me want to smile. She's throwing my words from Tuesday back at me, and I kind of like it. "Also, you look like hell."

I like that significantly less.

I *know* I look like hell. But the genius bodybuilder supermodel doesn't have to throw it in my face.

"Yeah, food poisoning," I explain, wiping the back of my hand against my mouth as we reach Jimmy's boat, *La Estrella Fugaz*. I have one foot on the hull when I feel Emily's hand around my elbow, pulling me back.

"Oh my god, you're sick? Why didn't you call me and cancel? You can't go on the water sick." Her expression is filled with so much genuine concern, and I think it's the first time since I saw my uncle, nearly ten months ago, that someone seemed like they cared if I lived or died.

"No phone, remember?" I reply, shaking her hand off my arm, fairly embarrassed that she can probably feel how gross and sweaty my skin is, even after my shower. "And it's just food poisoning, I'm not contagious."

"I'm not worried about you getting me sick," she says, her eyebrows furrowed. "Won't the waves make you feel worse?"

I scoff at the thought as I climb into the boat, reaching my arms out to signal for her to slide me the equipment. I can't lift those black boxes, but I'm strong enough to maneuver them as gravity does most of the work for me.

"I'm more at home on the water than I am on land," I reply honestly, feeling steadier even now as the soft waves of the harbor rock the boat. "And the sea air is good for you when you're sick."

Emily stands with her hands on her hips, her expression disbelieving. Despite the fact that I was desperate to crawl back into bed only an hour ago, I'm now glad I don't have a phone. I probably *would* have called to cancel or reschedule. But I would have missed this—talking to someone like I'm not a criminal on the lam.

I might be putting Emily at risk by spending so much time with her. Actually, I'm certain I am. And it's probably immoral, maybe even evil, to want to spend *more* time with her, and to be even more forthcoming about who I am. It could get her killed.

But as she surveys me up and down, I can't help but think that this is the last person on Earth who I might be able to truly get to know. Even if I succeed in my ludicrous plan, I'll likely be dead at the end of it. And if by some miracle I'm not, I'll be running and hiding for the rest of my life.

This charming, smart, seemingly perfect woman doesn't deserve to die because I crave the comfort of being known. But I've always felt more free on the water, and she asks so many questions. It's a perfect storm, and one I don't want to fight. I want someone to remember me. I want someone to have known who I was.

I can't tell her everything. I'll still have to lie more than I want to. But as she rolls her eyes and starts loading the equipment onto the boat, as the remnants of rattlesnake venom both destroy and fortify me, I realize I want to be Alisa for just a little bit longer.

Until she has to die again.

Chapter 6
Emily

I've been keeping a log of all the lies and truths Alice has told me.

I moved from Estonia about six years ago. Partially true. The *where* is a lie, obviously, but her timeline is not. I imagine she chose Estonia as her cover because her mother was from there.

She passed away when I was a child. Also true. I didn't push for details there, though I'm curious if she knows how much of a hand Konstantin had in her death. It would be uncouth and suspicious for a stranger to pry about the circumstances, though.

My father died in a car accident last year.

She's created a persona of emptiness. A woman with no one, nowhere, nothing to hold onto.

I'm surprised by how many of the things she tells me I can't categorize. Did she really learn English from her nanny and grow up fluent? I know she spoke English, Russian, and Mongolian by the time our paths crossed, but did she grow up learning them all in tandem? Is her biggest fear truly snakes? Is strawberry actually her favorite ice cream flavor?

Every minute with her is a reminder that my infatuation with her all these years was built on nothing but my imagination.

She's witty. Not quick to laugh, like I imagined she would be when I watched a recording of her giggling behind a delicate hand at something Ilya said. But she catches onto every slip of the tongue, every opening for a double entendre or barb. The more we talk, the less she openly smiles. But working for the tiny twitch in her deadpan expression is much more of a gift than the grins she shares with patrons.

She's also wildly brave. Once she allowed the dam holding back her personality to split a little, it became obvious why she was flabbergasted by my fear of...well, everything. When the ROV signal became compromised, she was the one who leaned over the side of the boat and hoisted the tiny machine back up so I could fix it. She told me about swimming in the open sea, jumping off high cliffs into the ocean below, even how she dreamed of SCUBA diving, which I told her was my version of Dante's seventh ring of hell.

I've tried to keep focus on my mission throughout our conversations, to ask her questions that help me understand her past and how it haunts her today. It'll take time to convince her to open up about some things though—especially her family. She gave me the barest details before clamming up and asking me about my past research.

The threat of Clara's clock ticks in the back of my mind every second of the day. I know I don't have time to lull Alice into a sense of security and friendship. Six weeks will go by in the blink of an eye, and then my hand will be forced.

Sitting on my bed, I watch the video feed as Alice leans her bike against the front facade of the grocery store. She doesn't go in, but walks around the side alley, filled with decaying cardboard boxes and broken beer bottles, to the ancient payphone near the dumpster.

Deniz pulled the call records before I even got here. Up until January, there were regular calls from this line to Mikhail Shevchenko, the long distance fee paid by the recipient. Since then, the calls are still placed every Friday evening. They all go unanswered.

Does she think her uncle abandoned her, or does she know her father well enough to suspect his involvement? Does she worry that her father discovered her drowning was fabricated?

Deniz has confirmed that not a single call has been placed from this payphone to anyone related to Konstantin, personally or professionally. In fact, the only calls made from that phone over the past year have been to Mikhail, other than two to a bail bond provider and one to a funeral home in upstate New York.

I haven't had a chance to sneak back over to place a recording device in the payphone, so for now I watch Alice as she feeds coins into the receptacle and dials the burner number that her uncle will never answer. Clara and Deniz are fairly certain that Konstantin isn't aware of the burner, but we likely will never know everything he pried from Mikhail's throat. We can only assume that if he knew about the calls from this payphone, Alice would already be gone.

When she finally gives in and hangs up, Alice walks back around the corner and into the store. The owner was watching me like a fucking hawk when I picked up groceries yesterday after I got off the boat, so I couldn't place any cameras inside. Which means now I'm antsy.

I shouldn't be watching Alice's every move anyway. My cousins are all pitching in with surveillance, reviewing record-ings and following up on anything potentially concerning. I should be doing what they can't—putting myself face to face with Alice.

Instead, I'll be doing anything but that.

It's my first non-research day, and I'm itching to be in her presence again. I've tried to convince myself the feeling is due to my creeping deadline, or my wholehearted dedication to The Syndicate's mission.

I suppose I'll have to create a list of lies I'm telling myself.

There's no gym in this town, but I need to burn off energy and I'm tired of fucking running. I've always preferred lifting, personally believing any cardio you do alone is a waste of time. There's a defunct playground a few miles inland, and I decide it's worth the risk to see if the rusting monkey bars can hold my weight.

I change into my standard workout gear—spandex shorts, a sports bra, and a MIT sweatshirt—and slip my headphones in. I never play music while I'm exercising, especially not when I'm running, but I like the way the noise cancellation mutes the outside world. I focus on my breathing and heart rate as I jog through the mist, my clothes immediately clinging uncomfortably as the humidity makes my skin slick. I hop the fence surrounding the abandoned RV park and jog to the advertised *community play area.*

The swings are broken, and the slide is filled with stagnant, mildewy water, but the monkey bars stand strong. Or so I hope.

The metal bites into my palms as I grasp the bar, shifting my weight and curling my legs up so they don't touch the ground on every rep. The calluses that my hands have grown accustomed to have softened a little in the last three weeks since I've been away from any real gym. But the pain is good. It centers me, focuses me, gives me something to think about other than reluctant smiles and pink-streaked hair.

My muscles stretch and burn as I pull myself up and let myself drop over and over, my body and mind controlled, organized, and obedient. Everything is conquerable. Fear, pain, lust, curiosity. Every emotion is a tool or a test that I will use or overcome. I am a Costa. I am cunning, strong, brilliant, and cutthroat. I *will* conquer this.

Whatever *this* is.

I drop to the ground and find a soft patch of dirt and grass. I usually hate getting dirty while working out, but there's something about holding a plank in the muck and getting pine needles in my hair as I do crunches that feels necessary right now. I need the distraction.

It's a sick twist of fate that I have actually enjoyed getting to know Alice. It struck me as we were sitting on that boat sharing the oranges I brought as a snack that if circumstances were different, we could have been friends. Maybe more. If Konstantin had been open to a partnership with The Syndicate, if we had become allies, if he had been a different man, perhaps we would have spent more time together. Aunt Lucia, and by extension Clara, maintains relationships with the families and enterprises we work with across the globe. Alice—well, *Alisa*—could have been one of them.

Instead, I'm learning about her with the sole intention of using her. And even if, by some miracle, I find a reason not to sacrifice her in the name of accessing her father, there's no way she'll ever forgive me when she finds out who I am.

All of these feelings—the guilt, the anticipation, the twisted sense of duty—would be tolerable, if it wasn't for the attraction.

It might be the only thing I got right in the fantasy I created about Alisa. Es una hermosura. Delicate and shimmering in the sunlight, her allure is only magnified by the little truths about herself that she lets slip every now and again. Not facts that I can write down in coded language in my research notebook. But inherent truths that we can't hide when we feel comfortable, and that we naturally conceal when we feel endangered.

Her humor, her bite, her inquisitiveness, her bravery. All of it makes the blue of her eyes brighter, the soft curve of her popped hip more enticing. The person I'm getting to know is so much better than the fantasy I created.

And I hate her for it.

It would have been so much easier to do what must be done if she wasn't...Alice. But she is, and the relief I had only a few days ago at being able to use her without guilt has been extinguished. Now I have to wonder if this brave and beautiful woman has built herself up from the crushing grip of her father's control, only for me to destroy her again.

Chapter 7
Alice

"Thanks Luanne," I say as the store owner shoves my meager haul into a thin plastic bag.

"No problem, sweetheart," she replies in her raspy smoker's voice. I've told her a thousand times I can bag my own groceries, but she refuses to let me.

"Where's Parker?" I ask as I pull slightly damp bills out of my pocket. The extra money from Emily's charter has been really helpful, even if I know Jimmy isn't cutting me anywhere near what is fair. I saw the dollar amount her program agreed to pay. Still, usually I'm doing math in my head in the aisles to make sure I don't go over budget, and it was nice not to have to today.

"Back with his dad for the school year," she says, melancholy seeping into her voice. I met Parker, Luanne's now-twelve year old son, last summer when I first got to Nesika Beach. He was surly and aloof, as most pre-teen boys are, but it was painful to see how much his mother wanted to spend time with him.

"July is a little early for back to school, isn't it?" She tries to smile as she takes my money, but it comes off as more of a grimace.

"He asked to go home early. Soccer camp."

I wish I could shake Parker. Tell him all the things I would give to have one last conversation with my mother. It's not fair to feel like that—I don't know Luanne's situation, there might be a good reason Parker doesn't want to spend time with her—but I can't help it. My grief over losing my mother has never faded. It's been almost two decades since I lost her, and time has not even begun to heal this wound. It's a gaping hole in my chest, raw and ragged and unendingly, excruciatingly painful.

I can still hear my mother's voice, like she's standing right next to me, every time I'm afraid. So when I see Luanne in pain over her distant son, I can't be objective.

The feeling only grows as I leave the store, hanging my bag on the handlebar of my bike and pushing off toward my apartment. This summer could have been the last time Luanne will ever see her son, and that is inarguably my fault.

Luanne, Jimmy, Alan, Paul who owns the pawn shop, Geneviene the bartender, Nigel the pastor, Willy and Dean who fish at the docks, Dominic the retired welder in his mobile home. It's impossible to know exactly how many people have lost their lives because of me, but in my worst nightmares these names are added to the list, next to my mother's and uncle's.

I have no idea who Ilya will kill to get to me. He doesn't see human life the way normal people do. Even his brother, who he probably cared for more than anyone else, was disposable to him. He was valuable because he was a tool for Ilya to use in his mad grab for power and influence. A fitting heir to my father's empire.

I was naive when I was young. I believed the story my father told me about my mother's drowning. How she went for a swim in the sea and the rip tide pulled her out unexpectedly.

He let me cry into his arms, said he would grieve her forever, just like me. He brushed my hair, like she used to, and told me all the stories about how they met and fell in love.

And then I never heard a word about her again.

I was only nine, but it felt like from that day forward, I was never a girl again. My father was both closer and more distant than ever before, giving me small glimpses into his work while simultaneously distancing himself emotionally. When I was thirteen, I started attending events with him. I thought it was because he trusted me, but really it was to show me off. To market the prize a lucky man would win if he could prove himself worthy of becoming heir to the most violent and cutthroat weapons runner in the world.

I was a signing bonus. A jewel some cruel man would fit onto his ring, fill with his children, and dispose of when I was no longer useful, the same as my mother before me.

For a while, it didn't bother me. Shamefully, I was even a little proud. I knew I was beautiful—my father told me constantly. He bought me dresses and jewelry and perfume to remind me of it. I went to language and music lessons, learned about Russian and international politics, was even taught about the weapons we traded in. I found, or perhaps desperately created, a sense of power in being the most coveted prize my father could offer. I wanted to be desired, even as a teenager. I was taught that it was the most important thing I could be, and I craved it more than anything except my mother's presence.

Until my father met Ilya.

The Andreeva brothers were newcomers to the scene, much like my father was when he started out. They were humble enough to earn their stripes as ground troops, but proved themselves loyal and useful, bringing in new clients and viciously extinguishing any threat to my father's success. Ilya in particular impressed him. Cunning, detached, motivated only by what he could gain. My father saw something moldable in him, and took him under his wing.

When I first met Ilya I was fourteen. He was twenty-two.

My father waited until I was slightly older to make his intentions known, but I saw the writing on the wall from that first meeting. Suddenly the fairy tale that I thought I would have, where someone strong and capable but who secretly wanted *me* more than anything else, came crumbling down around me. Even at our first meeting, Ilya cared nothing for me. He was curt and polite, but more interested in my father's lessons than any allure I provided. For a while I tried to change that. At a painfully young age, I flirted with him, tried to make myself into the type of young woman my father's commanders married. Nothing affected the blank way he started at me.

When I brought it up to my father, he said Ilya was being respectful of my young age. That he would show more interest when I was a woman instead of a girl. But when I did turn sixteen, the only thing Ilya wanted to do was control me.

Marriage into the Zakharov family was his key to my father's empire, and he was going to ensure that I did not compromise his future. My lessons stopped almost immediately. The clothing I was presented with became more conservative. The hallways and paths I used to sneak from my father's estate to play music in bars or drink in parks with strangers were sealed. I was shut out from meetings, given less and less knowledge about the operations of my father's business. I was isolated from the world, save from the few times Ilya handed me a dress and told me to be ready for a dinner where I would sit silently and demurely next to him.

Even then, I tried. I didn't know any other life. I convinced myself that my parents loved each other, and my mother did these things for my father, so it would work out. Ilya's ice would thaw, and he would show compassion. Not love, that would be asking for too much. But respect. Maybe, if I was lucky, desire.

It didn't matter that I wasn't attracted to him. Love was something you chose, and I could choose this. For my father, for his empire, for the memory of my mother.

The resentment began to build. An accumulation of so much indifference in the wake of my mother's ever-present love. The way Ilya's hands tightened around my arms when we were in public to control the pace of my steps, and how my father shrugged when he saw the bruises and said I would eventually learn to read my husband so well he wouldn't have to direct me. Seeing the few friends I still spoke to, the daughters of other commanders and messengers and footsoldiers, fall in love.

But I didn't break. Not until Ilya truly put his hands on me.

After my engagement, when my mother's family started slipping me notes through the chefs and housemaids and drivers under my father's employ, I knew the window to escape this life was closing quickly. As soon as Ilya had me under his roof, I would never have the opportunity again.

So I died. It's been years of paying in cash and moving towns under the cover of darkness. I've taken buses and trains and even boats, all at the direction of my uncle, who promised to keep me safe as an apology for not granting the same grace to his sister.

I'm certain he's dead now. Another casualty to add to the endless list of people who died so I could live in fear, hiding in abandoned towns and big cities, remaining unnoticed.

When I pull up to my apartment, I realize that only muscle memory got me home, but that isn't anything new. I often find myself lost in the blood of those who died for me even though I never asked for it. I lean my bike under the window outside my unit and contemplate the new name I have to add to the list.

Emily Vargas is the mostly likely collateral damage to my eventual discovery. We spend so much time together now, it's impossible to think Ilya won't have some interest in her. More than anyone else, the guilt over her inevitable death gnaws at me. Probably because I've come to peace with the fact that I chose this place. I knew when I started making my presence more obvious—letting my accent slip in towns friendly to my father's business, not keeping my face covered when I bought my bus ticket here, placing calls from the payphone to a bail bondsman I know Ilya once had under his surveillance—that I was accepting responsibility for whatever happened to these people. If any god existed, I'm sure he damned my soul long ago. But coming to terms with how many might become unintended casualties, even accepting them as means to the ends of my plan, put the final nail in the coffin of my fate.

Emily feels different. She shouldn't be here. She wasn't a part of my calculation. And she could have picked anywhere on the western coast of the United States to study her ridiculous fucking jellyfish, but she wound up here. Spending hours and hours with me.

She could have lived if she stayed away.

But I can't control that now. There's no saving her, and there's likely no saving myself. Even if my plan works absolutely perfectly, I will likely be dead by the end.

Mechanically, I put away my paltry groceries, ignoring the roar in my stomach and sitting on the floor at the foot of my futon. Hunger, shame, remorse, attraction—they all roil in my gut, making me more nauseous than the sea or rattlesnake venom ever has. I draw my knees to my chest and lay my forehead on them, blocking out the fading sun with my curtain of hair.

Even though I haven't felt this way about anyone else in this town, I feel this unignorable draw to do something for her.

Even though it's impossible, I want to make up for the fact that she will likely die before me. I want her to live as much as possible in these days or weeks or months before Ilya finds me, and consequently her.

I want her to feel free of the fear that plagues her, that lives in her like a virus. I want her to feel weightless in the middle of the ocean, and to see the majestic whales when they leap from the surface. I want her to see the whole world beneath our hull.

I want her to live before I cause her death.

Chapter 8
Emily

"**I** need to bring a final item to order."

Lucia's voice is so much stronger than the last time I saw her in person, at Charlie and Gwen's wedding. She smiles wider, laughs easier, allows her scars to be seen.

But there's an exhaustion in her eyes we've all been pretending doesn't exist.

"With the engagement of my eldest daughter, the time has come to pass the Matriarchy of The Syndicate of Fate to the next generation," Lucia says, tension visibly dissipating from her shoulders as she says the words. "Clara has been training for years for this, and with her partner by her side, she will be an unstoppable force in carrying out our mission."

I have no idea how much the current Matriarch knows about the circumstances of her daughter's engagement, but I doubt she has the full picture. Even Charlie, Gwen, Bea, and I have a limited understanding of the manipulation and mayhem that resulted in the vision before us—Clara and Deniz, seated side by side, her hand wrapped in his and displaying the stunning engagement ring that once belonged to Deniz's mother. For a while I believed that I was the *most* in the know, considering I dug up the information Clara used to blackmail Deniz into this marriage. But the events of this spring, and Deniz's surprise connection to Konstantin, have made me certain of only one thing—Clara will never tell any of us the full story.

It's enough to know that Konstantin is the reason Lucia has those scars. His attempt on her life in Istanbul over two years ago started the chain reaction of lies, vengeance, retribution that led us to this moment. Each of us may be going about it a different way, but we all have the same goals—take over for our parents by assuming our formal roles in The Syndicate of Fate, kill Konstantin and anyone else who believes they can attack our family without consequence, and remind the evil in this world that there is always someone out there hunting them.

Welcome to the Costa family.

"The official transition will be finalized after Clara and Deniz's wedding this winter, but we will be transferring internal coordination over in the meantime," Lucia continues, Aurelio's arm slipping over her shoulder. "We look forward to the success of your reign, Clara."

It's barely perceptible, but there's a slight wobble in Clara's serene smile as she thanks her mother. I can't say I blame her. She's starting off her oversight of The Syndicate in less than ideal circumstances, barely surviving a shootout a few months ago and still chasing an invisible mole in our ranks. None of us feel comfortable, especially knowing the world can see a weakness in The Syndicate of Fate. We all worry they'll take advantage of the vulnerability that Konstantin has shined a harsh light on.

Lucia closes the meeting, but I stay logged in to the encrypted video platform, waiting for the familiar notification to light up the screen. It doesn't take long.

I connect to the meeting to find my parents sitting side by side, their postures much more relaxed. I can hear the sounds of the city outside their windows, Buenos Aires already well into its day while the Pacific coast is still tucked in bed.

"Mi zorroito," my father greets brightly, using my nickname from childhood, gifted to me by Lucia. *Sveglio come una volpe,* she would whisper to my parents as I excelled in logic and reasoning, even more so than Clara. My father hasn't stopped calling me a fox ever since, even though we all know the rest of our world considers me more of a snake. "¿Cómo te va la investigación?"

I cringe internally at the double entendre. My parents believe I'm in western Oregon for my PhD research only. While I'm sure they assume we haven't dropped the investigation into Lucia's attack, as far as I'm aware, they know nothing about Lev or Clara's near-death experience or that Alisa Zakharov is still alive.

"Lento," I admit, nervously dragging my hands through my hair. "The nettles are hard to find, so understanding how their shifting habitat affects their toxicity to prey is going to take a long time. I'll be surprised if I even locate them by the end of the grant period."

Dr. Devenigh will likely murder me if that's the case, but we'll burn that bridge when we come to it.

"Paralytics aren't usually your area of focus," my mother says lightly, as if her tone will hide the trap in her words. "Did Dr. Devenigh provide any reasoning for such a change?"

In moments like these, it's obvious that my mother was raised a Costa, while my father only married into this life of subterfuge and hidden meanings. Unlike her sisters, who agreed to semi-arranged marriages with men from other criminal enterprises, my mother fell in love with a longshoreman and artist from Rosario. He accepted her and The Syndicate in every way to be able to spend his life with her, but he still has an artist's soul.

"You know how these things go, Mama," I reply just as casually, flipping through my notebooks on the desk beside me. "Grant funding changed, the deans shifted administrative focus. I need to graduate, I don't ask too many questions."

She knows I'm lying, and my father likely does too, but they don't push. We lie to each other all the time, it's inevitable in this life. In fact, my mother was the one who taught me to be strategic about the truth, to understand the value and vulnerability in honesty.

We catch up like we do after every Syndicate council session, only bringing up topics we can be honest about. They tell me about the work they're doing in Buenos Aires to garner more support from the local government in reducing trafficking. I tell them how jealous I am that they went home without me.

I was born in Bari, as all Costa descendents are. But I spent a lot of my upbringing traveling around Argentina with my father. It was the counterpoint to my strict, scheduled, and callous education in Italy, which was filled with everything from longitudinal algebra to torture lessons. But in Argentina, my father reminded me of the world my mother's family wanted to protect. Architecture tours in Córdoba, history lessons in San Miguel de Tucumán, penguin spotting in Punta Tombo, and once I was old enough, wine tastings in San Juan and Mendoza. We'd watch artists paint and listen to singers croon on the streets of Buenos Aires, and it stretched muscles that became stagnant under the tutelage of the Costas.

I haven't been back as often as I'd like in my adulthood. As the youngest of my generation of Costas, I've always felt like I was catching up to my cousins, leaving little room for walks down memory lane. Plus, being in school basically my entire adult life keeps one quite busy.

"Two Costa weddings in less than a year," my mother muses suddenly, her eyebrow arched. "I've always been sad I didn't inherit the tight curls of the Costa women, especially now as they flow around my mother's shoulders like twisting little rivers. "Perhaps it's time you started looking for a partner yourself."

The suggestion catches me off guard. My parents have never pushed for me to get married. There's no pressure to do so—I'm fourth in line for the seat of power in The Syndicate, and while Clara and Charlie have to marry to take their official roles as Matriarch and Hand, advisors like Bea and I do not.

"I haven't exactly had time to date," I hedge, looking to my father for support, who has his lips pressed into a straight line. I'm not sure if he's trying to hold back a laugh or not.

"You're around dozens of highly intelligent women every day, there has to be someone who has piqued your interest."

Unbidden, the image of Alice steering the boat, her baseball cap shading her eyes and a pink-streaked ponytail whipping in the wind flashes through my mind. I'm saved from having to respond by my father muttering *Alessia* under his breath.

"What, Mauricio? She is nearly thirty years old, it's time for her to think about this."

"First of all, I'm twenty-eight. That's not *nearly thirty*." My mother rolls her eyes, which is unfortunately fair, since my twenty-ninth birthday is in a few short weeks. "Second, I am currently in a town of four-hundred people, most of whom have at least fifteen years on me. Maybe this is something we should approach when I'm back in civilization."

Alice's reluctant grin flashes in my mind again, and I shake it from my head as my mother clicks her nails on the table beneath her laptop, the sound reverberating unpleasantly.

"That Rariny sharpshooter is single, isn't she? What's her name Mauricio?"

"Soa, I think," he answers, shooting me an apologetic glance through the screen.

"That's right, Soa. She's made quite a name for herself lately. You'd be a good match."

"I'm sorry, are you playing matchmaker now?" I ask, completely bewildered. For all their flaws, all three daughters of The Syndicate—my mother, Lucia, and Gia—agreed to allow their children to find partners of their own, a privilege they were mostly denied. My mother had to fight tooth and nail to marry my father, and it was only really allowed because she was the spare, second in line to the Matriarchy. "Of all people..."

"We're not playing matchmaker, mi zorrito," my father placates, even as my mother huffs next to him. "We know your mind has been elsewhere, and thought we could help push you in the right direction."

My knee-jerk reaction is to ask what the *right* direction would be, exactly. But I take a few deep breaths and try to remember that they love me.

"If I promise to think about seriously dating when I finish my dissertation, can we stop talking about this?" I beg, donning my most pleading smile and aiming at my father. He's always been easier to sway. I love him so much.

"Fine," my mother relents, her tone dulling as my father rubs small circles on her back. "We only pry because we know how hard this world is on one's own. Clara and Charlie have found people they can rely on. People they can tell the whole truth to without fear. You deserve that too."

Once more against my will, freckled cheeks and bright blue eyes flash in my mind, and I hate myself for it. Because Alice is the last person in the world I can be completely truthful with. And that shouldn't hurt as much as it does.

"You're in a weird mood today."

Alice's voice snaps me out of the spiral that was distracting me from even the horrors of the deep. We're bobbing gently on the ocean's surface, endless nothingness reflected on the ROV monitor as it always is. I've been staring off into space, trying to imagine myself married to Soa Raokoto. She's more a colleague than a friend, but we've gotten along well enough when we've crossed paths, and the Rariny share a similar moral compass to The Syndicate of Fate, if not more localized. My mother wasn't wrong when she said she's made a name for herself. No one alive can hit a target at the distances she can. Her kills have been publicly attributed to military drones. She's also, of course, exceptionally pretty, with bright eyes and a smile like a siren. Of course my parents would think her a good match for me.

By all reasoning, I *should* consider her. My mother wasn't wrong—this life is hard alone. Knowing that everything you hear, and even some things you see with your own eyes, may be a trick, lie, or manipulation really takes a toll on someone. You need a person to confide in, who helps you parse fiction from reality.

The problem is that every time I try to imagine Soa or some other faceless woman sitting next to me, my mind wanders to the woman I'm sharing a boat with.

I thought I was past this. The simple bubble of a childhood crush popped on day one, and I was able to see Alice as nothing more than a tool or pawn.

Then *why* does her face keep appearing in my mind when I think of confessions in the dark?

It has to be because of the situation we're in. Between my need to drag the truth out of her and our mutual lying and manipulation, wires have likely gotten crossed. I need her confession for utility's sake, to unearth something we can use against Konstantin, but with heightened emotions in play, it's natural that my desire for her to trust me has been mistaken by my heart for something more.

"Emily?"

When I turn to Alice, she actually looks concerned, which shouldn't be surprising. I probably seem halfway to catatonic.

"Sorry, just stressed," I say, harkening back to our conversation last week. At least that isn't a lie—I *am* stressed. More than I ever have been, if we're being honest.

"About the jellies?" she asks, reminding me that I should probably be watching the monitor more closely. "What happens if you don't locate them up here?"

"I probably will relocate a little further south and see if the warmer waters make them easier to find," I admit, wondering how long my dissertation process will take if that's the case. Identifying the location on the nettles is only the first step in this process. Then the actual research around the environmental impacts to toxicity begins.

"Oh." The broken and delusional part of my brain that's been picturing Alice as my trusted confidant imagines disappointment in that little word. "Well, you should see more while you're here. Live a little."

I raise my eyebrow at her, feeling painfully like my mother while I do it.

"See more of Nesika Beach? I think we can see it all standing in front of the discount store."

She deadpans, and I'm disappointed my joke didn't crack

her exterior. I've started thinking about Alice like Crème Brûlée, so convinced that there's something sweet and delightful under that little shell.

"Well we certainly don't have all the trappings of a big university town, I'd think you'd be surprised what adventure you can find here."

I *know* I'm imagining the undertone to her words. She didn't say them so they'd skate along my skin, leaving escalofríos and a buzzing sensation in their wake. Her expression gives away nothing.

"You going to take me on an adventure, Pecas?"

And finally, I get a smile.

Chapter 9
Alice

"You're gonna love this!"

She's actually going to hate this. But I'm convincing myself she'll live long enough to eventually appreciate the experience.

My resolve to help Emily live without fear has only grown over the weekend, as I worked the whale-watching cruises and caught glimpses of her on the shore, staring out at the water like it could swallow her whole. The guilt eating me alive demands recompense, and apparently my compensation for an early death is whales.

Also, whatever she called me in Spanish has my whole body vibrating like a tuning fork.

I push the boat faster, relishing in the hum of the engine and the way it rattles my whole frame through the steering wheel. Emily's sitting in the seat beside me in the small cockpit, her face a shade of green I've never seen on a human being before. I can't help the laugh that bursts out of me when she turns to me and smiles like she's being forced at gunpoint.

I check my coordinates on our GPS again, looking for the unique little dip in the continental shelf that we visit so often on our whale watching excursions. The deep, cold water means there's tons of zooplankton that travel up the water column from their frigid homes to feed on the phytoplankton near the surface. Where there are zooplankton there are the krill and other crustaceans who feed on them.

And where there are krill, there are whales.

We're in the middle of peak humpback migration season, with pods making the long journey down from Alaska to Hawaii to spend the winter in warm waters, giving birth to two-ton babies. These little pockets of cold water are the best places to find them fueling up for their nearly five thousand kilometer expedition.

When we get close, I slow the boat down, to Emily's relief. I pull the binoculars slung around my neck up to peer through and scan the horizon. Usually I'm nervous about finding them —we certainly don't on every whale watching cruise, much to our paying patrons' dismay—but I've got a good feeling about today. The ocean is on my side, I'm certain about it.

"Are you finding me new places to look for nettles? Because my research plan—"

"Will you be quiet?" I cut her off, the rubber of the binoculars pressed firmly around eyes. "No more nettles today."

"No nettles? Alice, I'm on a research grant, I have to—"

This time I cut her off with a slap to the arm. She must be as surprised by the action as I am, because it effectively shuts her up. I shake my hand, willing away the feeling of her sun-warmed skin before latching on to the binoculars again.

They only really hold their breath for about ten to twenty minutes while they're feeding. So it shouldn't be long. Any moment now I should see...

"There," I breathe, slipping the cord from around my neck and handing the binoculars to Emily. "Watch right there."

She follows my direction, one hand still in a death grip on

the front railing, peering through the binoculars while I creep the boat toward them. We're not too far, and I don't want to drive them away with the sound of the engine, so I let the boat coast when we get close enough, the ocean itself drawing us toward the whales.

"Holy shit," Emily whispers, and a sense of pride and possibly smugness floods my chest. My instinct is to shut it down, to downplay. But fuck that, *I* brought her here to witness these incredible creatures.

"I know, right?" I say, gently pushing the binoculars away from her eyes. "We're close enough now."

I swear her cheeks heat a little as she lets them fall.

In a predictable, wonderful cycle, the humpback whales in front of us feed. Their rostrums slip gently above the water, gliding along until their blowholes are exposed. The puff of their breath is so loud this close, the mist dissipating quickly into the sunlight. As they arch to dive back into the sea, their white-spotted spines lift and curl, giving them the momentum to push their enormous bodies further into the ocean's depths to find their meal.

At the last moment, right before they sink beneath the waves, their flukes sometimes lift above the surface.

"They're waving."

I was so caught up in watching my favorite animals on the face of the planet, I almost forgot Emily was right beside me. When I turn to her, her face reflects what I heard in her voice—pure, unadulterated joy. Her eyes are saucer-wide, her lips parted like she knows there are no words to describe what she's seeing. She's not even holding the railing anymore, her hands hovering in front of her like she's trying to reach out and touch them.

"They use the momentum from lifting their flukes to propel themselves deep into the water," I explain, my voice barely above a whisper as the smallest of the pod—about four or five years old—starts his cycle at the surface.

"I'm gonna pretend they're waving," she replies, unable to peel her eyes away from the sight in front of her. I bury the smile pulling at the corners of my mouth. Emily is already strong, smart, and beautiful, I cannot also find her charming.

We watch for a few more minutes as the rest of the pod, four in total, dives beneath the surface. I know there will likely be a gap where they travel deep in the water, so I dig my sunglasses from the drawstring bag at my feet.

"Here," I say, handing her a spare pair that I nabbed from the lost and found at the end of last season. "The polarization helps you see them underwater."

Together we watch the surface, the silence comfortable yet tense as we try to anticipate where the whales will pop up next. Emily sees them first this time.

"Over there?" she asks, like she's unsure. Like she's deferring to me and my expertise. I kick the boat back on and slowly make our way in the direction of the blows.

"Good spot," I say, tapping my elbow to her arm. Her smile is genuine when she looks at me, keeping her arm pressed to mine in an agonizing moment of contact. I'm both thankful for and pissed as hell when one of the whales lunges, pulling our attention.

Their mouths jut from the surface, opening like claws and swallowing mouthfuls of water before sinking back below, like a bobbing buoy. The birds have started to join us, clusters of them diving for the same meal as their underwater dinner partners.

"Do they swallow all of that?" Emily asks, her stomach now pressed to the helm as she leans toward the scene in front of us.

"Humpbacks are baleen whales, which means they have long filaments instead of teeth," I explain, like I do on the tours nearly every day. "They'll grab a mouthful of krill and small fish, and then expel the water through the filament, trapping their meal inside."

"Fascinating," Emily says, seeming genuinely impressed. And who wouldn't be? These are some of the largest animals on the planet, consuming tons upon tons of some of the *smallest* animals on the planet.

I've been trying to track the members of the pod, but they're not the group that has been hanging out here the last few weeks, so the markings are unfamiliar. But I have noticed that only three of the whales seem to be popping up for air right now. Which I hope means something spectacular is about to happen.

"Keep your eyes up, look wide," I instruct, and Emily straightens out, taking everything I say seriously. I press my lips together, trying not to laugh. My chest is so full I feel like it could burst at any moment. I may not be able to show her much, but at least she's not afraid right now.

Maybe it's pattern recognition, or I've been doing this so long that the ocean recognizes me, knows I respect and love her. Because instinctually, I grab Emily's hand and point toward a spot about twenty yards to our starboard, around three o'clock.

Right at that point, the smallest humpback launches himself from the ocean.

Emily audibly gasps as he arches from the surface, turning his body sideways and crash landing back into the water with an outsized splash. The waves rock the boat harder, and Emily reaches out with her free hand to grip the railing again. Which makes me realize I'm still holding her other hand.

She looks down at me, her smile so open and wide I swear I've never seen anything as beautiful. She laces her fingers with mine like she doesn't even notice she's doing it, her body shaking with silent laughter.

"What was that?" she asks incredulously, her tone so much higher than usual, coated in disbelief of what she saw with her own eyes.

"A breach," I respond, my voice a little caught in my throat. "There's lots of reasons we think they do that, but I like to believe that they're playing with us. And each other."

She's not looking at the whales anymore. She's watching my lips as they form my reply, and then her gaze sinks down to where our hands are interlocked before finding my eyes again.

"Thank you for taking me on an adventure, Pecas," she mutters, her body suddenly so much closer to mine. That buzzing feeling is back, so much different than the adrenaline of seeing the whales. It's like I've been electrocuted, and the current runs through her fingertips. I wonder what they would feel like all over my body, shocking me alive over and over again.

I get a taste of my daydreams. She lets go of the railing and drags her hand across my hip, pulling me gently even closer to her, using the motion of the waves to her advantage. I can feel her touch like a live wire through my clothes, and my vision becomes hazy with something that feels suspiciously like lust.

That guilty feeling of attraction to someone not pre-selected for me still lives deep in my chest, nipping at me. But I think whatever monster makes me feel that way is shocked into submission by Emily's touch, especially when she drags her hand slightly higher, the motion exposing a sliver of my midriff. Her skin directly on mine makes the small hairs on my entire body stand on end, and I know she notices.

"Are you afraid right now?" I ask, because I honestly can't tell. But over the past week, I've realized she enjoys it when I bite back at her questions or reply to hers with a cutting remark. She likes the fight, and I want her to like me right now.

Even if that's a terrible idea.

"Of the ocean?" she asks, her touch slightly higher now, skating against the bottom of my ribcage. The little smile on her lips tells me she knows that's not what I'm asking.

"Yes, of the ocean," I breathe, trying to maintain my composure. Part of me hates that she's so in control, so seemingly unaffected, while I can feel my bones being rattled by her touch. But the other part of me doesn't hate it at all. That other, smaller, louder part of me desperately craves to feel vulnerable around someone who won't take advantage of it. Who I know will take care of everything without seeing me as weak for it.

For some reason, like the delusion of a wretched, dying animal, I've come to believe Emily could be that for me.

"I think you've cured me," she says, her hand now at the small of my back, like she's a hair's breadth away from lifting me closer to her. "Right now, I'm not afraid of anything. Are you, Pecas?"

Against my better judgement, I lift myself up onto my toes and bring myself closer to her, watching her eyes turn hungry. *This is what attraction is supposed to look like*, I think to myself as she scans my face, tracing every dip and line.

"Maybe I like being a little afraid of you." Even though it's true, I'm not sure when I realized it. There's something alluring about the fact that she is stronger and smarter than me, that if she wanted to, she could hurt me. That she *doesn't* want to. I'd put all the money in my pocket on the belief that hurting me is the last thing in the world Emily wants to do.

It's delusional. Certainly naive. But I want to believe it so badly that I see it written all over her face.

She leans down, so much taller than me it must be an inconvenience. My eyes flutter closed when she's only a breath away, her lips so close to mine I can feel the heat of them. Everything else has faded away, and the places where we're touching, or almost touching, are the only things that exist. The sound of her breath and my own heartbeat are the only things in my ears.

It hits me that I want her to touch me. Not just a kiss, not just a brief touch of skin. Those are things I shared with Ilya. I want more—I want what he never wanted to take, even when I offered. What I've had with no one else.

If I'm going to die, I want to *want*. And to be wanted in return.

Emily's so close, her lips brushing mine like she's savoring every second. Her hand is pressed firmly into my back now, so steady and warm. On instinct, I run my tongue along the back of my teeth, a nervous habit.

And stop.

"Wait," I say, slipping my fingers from hers and stepping back. She straightens immediately, moving further away from me as well.

"I'm sorry," she immediately says, her hands going behind her back like she's punishing herself. "We're working together, I shouldn't have..."

"No," I cut her off, trying to figure out how I'm going to get around this particular issue. She can't kiss me, even though I want it more than most things I've wanted in my life. "I just... I've never kissed someone before."

The lie slips out easily, like the dozens of others I've told her, but it feels worse. It sits in my stomach like a little lead ball, rolling around and filling me with poison.

Emily's face is understandably shocked. We're about the same age, and I imagine she's plenty...experienced. The thought makes my skin feel sunburnt.

"You've..."

"Never been kissed, yeah, I know it's strange," I rush out, trying to use the pieces of truth I've allowed from my past to fill in a backstory. "I was sheltered, and my parents were very strict. I've been pretty isolated since I moved to the States."

"Oh, okay I guess that makes sense," she says warily, running her hand through her hair. The lightning feeling from before comes back when her gaze snags on my exposed hip, from where her hand was. "I apologize if I pushed too far."

No, please, push further, I want to say aloud. I don't know how to get her to keep touching me without kissing her. Because I don't want to give up the feeling of her skin on mine, but I also don't trust myself not to kill her if she kisses me. I fear that, with her mouth on mine, I might accidentally break the capsule of rattlesnake poison hidden in a false cap in my back molar that's saved for someone special.

The pleasure of dying by my lips is for Ilya alone.

"I liked it," I say, my voice desperate as I take a step closer to her. She's cautious with her gaze now, but I still catch her looking at my lips. I know what indifference looks like. Emily is not indifferent to me. "I liked how it felt when you touched me."

I take one step closer to her, nerves and guilt and anticipation building in my stomach as she lets me draw nearer. Apparently I'm going to ask everything of Emily. To be the only person I tell my truths to. To have her be the first and last person to touch me. To die because of me.

Назвался груздем - полезай в кузов.

"Did you?" she asks. I can't tell if she's really unsure, or she's pressing me to admit more.

"I did," I admit quietly, reaching for her hand and gently placing it back on my exposed skin. Her fingers flex like she feels the electric current too.

"Do you want me to touch you more?" Emily asks, her

hand completely still as she waits for my reaction. I nod, victory sweeping through my chest as she moves closer.

"And you don't want me to kiss you?"

I shake my head and she leans down again, her mouth so close to mine I consider taking the risk and hoping I have more control than I know I do.

"Just your mouth?" she asks, and I don't move, because I'm not sure what she's asking. She waits a few beats. "Am I allowed to kiss you anywhere else?"

The electric current is so strong I feel myself shaking, but that's not what makes me nod yes. It's the thought of Emily's mouth anywhere, everywhere. She's so methodical, so exact. I wonder how she'd be with my body as the research subject.

I really hope I'm about to find out.

Chapter 10
Emily

Alice lied.

Not a lie like all the others before. Not to keep herself safe, not to obscure her past. It's a lie I don't understand the motive of.

I've seen her kiss Ilya dozens of times, in recordings and through live feeds. Chaste, lustless kisses, sure, but I imagined that was Alisa's preference. I assumed that their engagement would have come with the modern physical expectations, regardless of how protective her father clearly was. I can't tell if she's simply lying about all her sexual experience, for some unimaginable reason, or just the kissing bit.

And right now, I really don't care.

If she doesn't want me to kiss her, I won't. But there are a thousand other things I can do to make her eyes drift closed like that. Virginity is a useless social concept, one I shed shortly after returning from Vladivostok that winter, but if Alice is being truthful about her lack of experience, I need to tread lightly. She's been through a lifetime of trauma in her twenty-seven years, and I'm still being more intimate with her than apparently anyone ever has before.

Coupled with the unavoidable truth that I should *not* be doing this, that I'm compromising my mission and my ability to see Alice as a target, that I might actually be risking my place in The Syndicate...this is complicated. So beyond complicated.

And again, I really don't care.

"What if I kiss you here?" I whisper, gently drifting my lips along the line of her jaw, tilting her head up for better access. Her skin tastes like the salt of sweat and the sea, with something sweeter underneath that I can't discern. I want to eat her alive so I can identify it.

"Mmmm," she hums, and my head swims with lust and hubris. I'm so confident that I can make that pretty sound come out of her again that I open my mouth against her skin, letting my tongue sweep the expanse that I kissed.

This new sound is even better. Shocked pleasure, something between a sigh and a cry that I chase it with more open-mouthed kisses across her throat. For some reason, the Act of Contrition plays on loop in my head as I nip at the place where her shirt lays against her collar. My family was understandably never religious, but I heard the prayers everywhere when I was in Argentina. I suppose if there was ever a sin I needed forgiveness for, touching Alice like this when I've lied to her about my entire life would make the top of the list.

Again...

"What about here?" I ask into her skin, dragging both my hands up her sides until my thumbs are right under her breasts. She grips my elbows, leaning against the console for support but digging her fingernails into my arms all the same.

"Please..." she whines, so fucking pretty I can feel my entire body lighting on fire. The sound of her begging stirs up a universe of things I could make her plead for. Things that will never happen, but I'll carry in my imagination long after our summer here is over.

"Please what, Pecas?" I taunt, shifting my thumbs in slow circles on the underside of her small breasts, barely avoiding what I know she wants.

"More," she breathes, her grip tightening before pulling me closer, surprising me. I'm reminded once again that the docile, sweet image of her I created in my head was nothing but a fabrication.

The way I need her reminds me I like this version so much better.

"You want more places I can kiss you?" I ask, barely giving her a moment before I push her higher against the console and slide my knee between her legs so she's straddling my thigh. Her eyes aren't fluttering closed anymore, but are wide open with blown pupils. I slide my hands down to her hips and ever so subtly rock her against me.

She let go of my arms in her surprise, and now she puts them behind her, supporting her weight against the helm as she follows my gentle guidance, rocking herself against my thigh. Even though her shorts and my cargo pants, I can feel how warm and wet she is, so fucking perfect and turned on only from these little touches.

"What about here, Alice?" I ask, rocking her harder against me to make my point. I'm convinced her breathy cries of ecstasy could make me come standing here. She adjusts herself on my thigh, finding the angle that brings her the most pleasure and chasing it. "Can I kiss you here?"

I would do just about anything to. I want to taste her summer sweetness on my tongue, to know what she looks like when she falls apart because of my mouth. I can't kiss her, can't make her taste herself from my lips, but I already know it'll be short work before I make her come on my fingers first and slip them in her mouth while I follow through with my own.

I'm teetering on a dangerous edge. I may have been rebellious in my teen years, but I've never put the mission of The Syndicate at risk before. Not for any partner, and certainly not for one I know I have no future with. But there's something about the way she pushes off the console and rises to her toes so she can rock herself harder on my leg that makes me want to follow her to the ends of the Earth.

"Answer me, Alice," I demand, rocking her hips with my hands faster than she can on her own. She's muttering incoherently, nothing but choked cries and pleas with my name buried between them.

"Yes, please," she cries, and I increase the pressure but not the pace of her movements against my thigh. Only a few rolls of her hips later, she tosses her head back, her hair falling in waves against the controls as she shakes and cries. I don't stop my movements, needing to prolong the sound of her pleasure in my head, already desperate to hear it over and over again.

Her orgasm lasts a lifetime, a gift from the universe that I won't soon forget. She lets me rock her body against mine until the final waves of it ebb from her. I lean over her to kiss up the column of her throat, the salt of her skin even sweeter now.

"Oh my god," Alice mutters, her head still hanging back, her chest rising and falling with heavy breaths. I like the way I can feel the vibrations of her words when my lips are on her neck.

"How are you feeling?" I ask, keeping her firmly supported on my leg, my hands unmoving from her hips. I remember all my firsts, and the most painful ones were those where I felt my partner withdraw quickly after the adrenaline died down. That's the one betrayal I can guarantee not to give Alice.

"That's so much better than when I do it myself," she murmurs, and at my soft laugh she slaps her hand over her mouth. "I was supposed to say that in my head."

There's not much that could inflate my ego further at this

moment, but I'm already impatient to touch her again. Her body is loose and languid, so pliant in my hands as I slip them under her shirt again.

"Emily..." she protests weakly, arching as my fingers find the soft skin under her chest again.

"Do you want me to stop?" I would, reluctantly, if she wanted me to. I get the impression that Alice feels a lot more uninhibited out here on the water than she does on shore, and I have no idea if I'll get another opportunity like this again.

When I pull my mouth from her neck, where I've been careful not to leave any marks, she finds my eyes. Still lust-steeped, still wanting, but a little more hesitant this time.

"You can stop anything at any time," I promise, taking my hands away from her body so we can both focus. "You say the word, and I swear to you, we stop immediately. There's no shame, no hard feelings. This is all new, and my priority is your comfort."

Something complex flashes in her eyes. Relief and interest, but threaded with something harsher. It's gone in an instant.

"What if I don't want you to stop?" she asks. It's the first time I've felt like she's actually flirted with me, her voice breathy and soft. It makes me want to give her anything she's ever wanted.

"Pick a word. Anything but *stop*. You say it, we break. That way you can beg me *not* to stop all you want."

She hesitates for a moment, her eyes scanning the boat and the horizon like she's trying to pick a safe word from her environment, which I find painfully adorable. Her gaze finally lands on my research equipment, a small grin tugging at the corner of her mouth.

"Jellyfish," she says, almost with a giggle. I can't help my own smile in return.

"Okay, Pecas. Jellyfish it is," I agree. There's a small ledge next to the steering wheel that I settle her on, lifting her weight off my leg so I can have better access to all the parts of her I want. "You say *jellyfish*, and I'll stop. Until then, I'm going to find all the places on your body I'm allowed to kiss. Understand?"

She braces herself again, her knees falling slightly open as she nods at me.

I don't waste another moment. Lifting the hem of her tee shirt and holding it near her collarbone, I kiss a line straight from her belly button to her sternum. Her breasts are still covered, and I take my time teasing the soft, pale skin of her stomach, the waistline of her shorts, the slight arch at her hipbone with two faded, parallel scars that I want to ask about.

The ocean rocks the boat, creating a tempo that Alice follows as she arches into me. Her soft sighs quickly melt into pleas, until I feel her fingers in my hair.

I've never been one to enjoy having my hair pulled. Generally I'm in the opposite role—controlling and giving, rather than submitting and receiving. But I'm coming to the very dangerous realization that I'd likely let Alice do whatever she wanted, if it made her come like that again.

I expect to find her expression supplicating, but instead she's demanding. Insistent. Impatient. She tugs my hair a little, sending skitters down my spine.

"Don't stop."

What Alice wants...

I tug her shirt over her head roughly, and the sunglasses she had pushed back into her hair go flying. I don't have time to care though, because a vision I've been dreaming of for far longer than I care to admit sits in front of me. Alice, messy and perfect and half undressed, barely-there freckles dancing along her skin and pale pink nipples hard and waiting for me.

I'm on my knees in front of her, my height places my

mouth directly in line with her tits, which I take full advantage of. I immediately pull one of her nipples into my mouth, rolling on the bud as I press a hand into the small of her back, forcing her to arch harder for me. The sounds of pleasure coming from her suddenly become muffled, and I glance up to see her covering her own mouth. Which obviously will not do.

I snatch her hand away with my free one, placing it on her own tit and squeezing. My hand is so much bigger than hers, it covers hers and her breast completely.

"Who are you being quiet for?" I ask, flicking her fully hard nipple with my tongue as she stares at me, mouth agape. "No one can hear you out here except me. And I want to *hear* you."

I don't wait for her to respond. I'm too consumed by the taste of her skin, the feeling of her delicate body leaning into mine, chasing her own pleasure. When I shift to give equal treatment to her other breast, she automatically switches hands, rolling the nipple I just had in my mouth between her fingers. I'd praise her for it if my mouth wasn't so preoccupied.

As beautiful as she looks like this, I know what both of us really need. I work on unbuttoning the fly of her shorts, the cotton thin and too loose on her frame, and keep my eyes on hers the whole time. There's a small bit of hesitation there, which is expected, especially if this is her first time.

It hits me all of a sudden that I am the first person to see her like this. Depending on how the next few weeks go, I may be the only person to *ever* see her like this. She is totally and completely mine. No matter how much we lie to each other, manipulate and avoid and obscure, that will always be true.

She doesn't stop me as I drag her shorts down and over her shoes, dropping them in the captain's chair beside me. Her plain cotton underwear are wet from her first orgasm and all the arousal of my mouth on her body.

"Anything you want to say?" I ask, my fingertips sliding under the elastic hem stretched across her ass.

That flash of defiance comes rearing back, and she lifts her own hips, sliding her underwear to the ground and forcing me backward on to my ass while she does it. She doesn't open her legs back up—I don't think she's quite that brave yet—but she leans back on her hands smugly and tilts her chin up at me.

"Don't stop," she replies with a smile.

Thank god.

I slide my hands under her thighs and pull them apart, so fucking hungry for her it feels like I'm starved. I want to go slow, to take my time and tease her and make her beg, but I've decided that this will not be the last time I get to touch her, if I have anything to say about it. I'll monopolize every second of the next five weeks of our time together to teach her to beg for what she wants, to pull her apart molecule by molecule and find all the touches and kisses that make her fall apart for me.

Trailing open-mouthed kisses up the inside of her legs, I inch closer and closer to her exposed pussy. She tried to arch toward me, to close her thighs in the face of all that tension, but I don't allow her to control this. Instead I take my time, skimming over the soft indents in her waistline where her clothes bit into her skin as I reach the apex of her thighs. Keeping her spread wide for me with my hands on her knees.

It doesn't take her long to start begging, whining my name, asking so sweetly for something she can't yet name. I'm already obsessed with the sound, with how easily her brattiness is tamed when she really wants what I can give her.

Finally, when I've traced each leg from hip to ankle with my mouth, I give her what she's begging for. What I'm begging for, too.

I drag my tongue from entrance to clit, savoring the taste of her, and the sound she makes when my mouth is finally on her.

"Fuck, Emily, oh my god," she breathes, her thighs instinctively drawing together around my head until I push them back open, forcing her to experience this pleasure at it's most raw.

"I know, Pecas," I placate, gently drawing circles around her clit with the hand not holding her thigh open. "So good for me."

She whines as her hips buck forward, and I tuck her reaction to praise in my pocket for later as I resume eating her, sucking on her clit and letting her find a pace she enjoys as she rides my face.

I hate that it's never been like this before. I hate that every moment of her pleasure and mine is built on lies and manipulation. But even more, I hate that I can't stop myself from swinging her thigh over my shoulder and reaching down to unbutton my own pants.

"Are you..." she stutters, the words choked off as I flatten my tongue directly on her clit for a moment. "Christ, are you touching yourself while you're...damn it, I don't know the term in English."

We both laugh, the sensation oddly perfect among all this tension and lust, and I slide my fingers against my own clit as I pull away from hers.

"The Americans call it *eating out*," I chuckle, and she shakes with her own laugh before I return to my work.

The build is a bit slower, but it somehow feels more connected, with my pleasure ratcheting up alongside hers. She doesn't hide her noises now, releasing gasps and sighs and whines that leave me rocking my clit against the heel of my palm with two fingers inside me. I grip her thigh over my shoulder for balance and move both of us to the rhythm she sets as she grinds against my face.

I can't wait to give her more. To see her take my fingers, to watch her grind against me while she's under my body, to witness her take toys until she's come in every manner I can think of. But right now, watching her fall apart from the feeling of my mouth against her...I'll never get over this.

"Emily," she cries, her hips grinding down harder against my face. I want to tell her I'm close too, but I'd rather die than move my mouth from where it is right now, so I squeeze her leg and increase the pressure on both our clits. Her movements become hurried and uneven, and I feel myself fall the moment before she does.

Coming with her, feeling her body break while it's connected with mine, is indescribable. I groan into her skin as she rides out her pleasure on my face, drawing my orgasm out longer than I would alone, so desperate for the moment not to end.

Finally, we're both spent. Alice leans all the way back against the console, her arms at odd angles to avoid the controls. I stand up and rebutton my pants, wiping the evidence of Alice's orgasm off my mouth with the back of my hand. She watches like she can't believe what she's seeing as I lick it clean, not wasting a drop of what she gave me.

She's nearly naked, save for her socks and tennis shoes. Her skin is turning pink under the glaring sun, either from its rays of the glow of her pleasure. But she looks over her shoulder, and the first thing she says to me...

"The whales are gone."

Chapter 11
Alice

I think I might be a bad person.

Most of my life, I was so sheltered from the world and my impact on it, it never occurred to me to contemplate my morality. I didn't even wonder if my father's work was right or wrong, even as I learned more about it in my teen years. This was just the way the world was, and I played my part in it. After that night with Ilya, when I realized I needed to escape, I was too focused on survival to consider if the scales would balance in my favor. I saw myself as a victim, someone who these things were happening *to* instead of a willing actor in a system of which I was finally experiencing the consequences.

Perhaps that should have been my first sign that I wasn't good. I thought of myself as helpless, and didn't consider the impact of my life and actions on the world until someone I cared about was on the receiving end of my karma.

But now I know where I stand. Because I know it's wrong to keep sleeping with Emily. I recognize that it puts this innocent, oblivious, brilliant woman in more danger. I understand that with each passing day I spend letting her teach me what I've been missing, I harden the seal on her death certificate.

But that doesn't seem to stop me from crawling back to her bed every day this week.

On the research days, we took the boat out to the coordinates she gave me, set up the ROV, and tried to remember to watch the monitor for hours at a time. On whale watch days, every second I wasn't on the catamaran, I spent with her.

I still haven't kissed her, even though it's all I want to do. I considered taking the capsule out while I'm at work, but I can't predict when Ilya will show up. It has to be soon. As much as my uncle cared for me, I'm certain my father would only grant him the mercy of death once he handed over the information he needed. Whatever Mikhail told him, coupled with the carefully placed hints I've left over the past few months, I know my time is short. Ilya could steal me from my apartment, or off the street, or in the damn discount store. The only place I feel safe is on the water, and I can't exactly explain removing a capsule of poison from my mouth to Emily. I have to keep it on my body at all times, so at the first opportunity, I can give Ilya exactly the end he deserves.

"Alice!"

I snap my head up, whipping around to find Alan holding a mop out to me. Once again, I was daydreaming about Emily's fingers in my...

"Are you going to help us clean or do you want to be here all night?" he scoffs, rolling his eyes at me. If *Alan* is complaining about my work ethic, I know it's gotten really bad.

"Yeah, sorry," I mutter, grabbing the mop from him and shuffling to the bathroom. It's the last cruise of the week, and on each one before this I've been wholly distracted. I'm actually thankful that we've sold zero tickets for our Monday cruises. No trips mean no pay, but it also means I get a whole day off, which I haven't had since Emily's research trips began.

I should take the opportunity to up my dose of poison

tonight, since I can risk being sick in bed all day tomorrow. Instead, I imagine I'll find myself in the only occupied room of the best motel in town again.

When the vessel is as clean as it will ever get, the three of us disembark, and I volunteer to haul the trash bags to the dump at the end of the lot. After I'm done, I rinse my hands in the grimy dock bathroom, fully planning on riding my bike directly to Emily's hotel room. But I'm surprised to find her waiting by the dock, leaning against the door of her rental car.

"What are you doing here?" I ask, drying my hands on my shorts as I approach her. She raises her eyebrows at me.

"Such a warm welcome," she scoffs, opening up the passenger door. "I thought you could take me on another adventure."

I'm not sure how I'll *take her* on an adventure from the passenger seat, but I shrug and slide in. Not like I know how to drive a car anyway.

"What kind of adventure would you like to go on?" I ask as she pulls the sleek little car out of the dock parking lot. There's a nervous smile playing at her lips.

"You said that you go cliff jumping," Emily hedges, her fingertips drumming against the steering wheel. "I know it's probably too late to do that now, but I thought we could sit on the cliff and watch the ocean and eat something."

She nods toward the back seat, where paper bags are filled with discount store snacks and takeout food from the burger place in Port Oxford.

"You went all the way up there?" I don't ask Emily what she does with her days when we're not tracking sea nettles. Partially because I assume she's working on her dissertation, compiling the data we collect or whatever, but also because it feels wrong to ask. I can't ask for more from her than what she's already giving. Knowing what she does when I'm not around would feel somehow more personal than all the intimacy we've shared, and would only serve to make my guilt worse.

"I finished the methodology portion of my dissertation, so we deserve to celebrate," she says with a little shrug, brushing off what I assume is a fairly significant achievement. Without my direction, she navigates the car off the main road and up one leading to a hiking trail. Well, more of a glorified dirt road with a faded wood signpost at the trailhead.

"You've been here before?" I ask as she parks along the side of the path, the car tilted slightly sideways on the slope.

"Googled it."

Right. Most people have computers and phones and internet access. Luxuries I do miss. Every once in a while I wonder how my favorite television series ended, or what music is popular in Vladivostok now. The only times I've been online since I left Russia were to book bus or train tickets at public libraries using prepaid gift cards.

Emily gathers the bags from the back of the car, refusing to let me help, before leading the way up the trail. This isn't the area I usually jump from—the rocks jutting up from the ocean are a clear enough warning to stay on land—but I have followed this trail before. It's peaceful, the thicket of trees buffering the sound of the ocean until you find their break. The sensation of stepping through the treeline is like raising a curtain on a stage. The entire world opens up in front of you, the murmuring of the crowd no longer muffled by red velvet, but filling your body like the crashing of the waves below.

The horizon is endless here. Emily sets up our dinner as close to the edge of the cliff as she probably feels comfortable, I stand a few feet closer, letting the adrenaline of the height flood my nervous system. It's a high that, before a week ago, I thought couldn't be matched. The hues of the sunset reflect on the surface of the water, the oranges and pinks bleeding like paint spilled on an eternal canvas. Golden sunlight flickers in the motion of the waves, shimmering like glitter. A beautiful, messy piece of art.

"I assume you're afraid of heights as well?" I ask as I turn back to Emily, blinking back the tears welling in my eyes. Sometimes I hate that this world has so many beautiful things, like the ocean and pistachio ice cream and blackberry mojitos and sunsets and Emily, and I get so little time with them.

"Falling from this height would be instantly fatal. I think this fear is both reasonable and healthy." If Emily notices my tears, she doesn't say anything. She pats the spot next to her on the blanket she's laid out for us.

"So are you afraid of heights, or afraid of falling?" I ask, joining her in front of our meal and crossing my legs beneath me. "Or maybe you're afraid of dying?"

A muscle twitches in her cheek, and I wish I could take the words back. I don't want to know if she's afraid of dying. I don't want to face the fact that, sooner rather than later, I'll likely be the one to force her to face that fear. That my selfishness will be the reason she will be afraid before she dies.

"I think dying is the only thing I'm *not* afraid of," she admits with a humorless laugh, and somehow that makes my guilt even worse. "It's inevitable. There's no point of being afraid of something you can't escape."

My tongue is stuck in my throat, and I stare at the ocean again to avoid her gaze. I can't say I agree. I'm afraid of lots of inevitable, inescapable things. Dying, sure, though I hope I might be lucky enough to see my mother again in whatever afterlife exists. Ilya finding me. Even though I'm prepared, and I know what I have to do, I can still hear his voice in my head telling me the words that pushed me to escape. I know seeing him will be terrifying, that he might torture me as punishment for embarrassing him, or on behalf of my father for my treason. I'm afraid of the unavoidable pain.

Before my mother's family gave me hope of escape, I was afraid of being trapped in that life. Of dying like my mother did, for the simple crime of no longer being useful to the man who owned me, and of being a liability to his ego. I thought I knew the course of my entire life, and it was terrifying.

I'm afraid of losing Emily, even though that is also an inescapable reality. Even if, by some miracle, she doesn't become collateral damage in Ilya's path toward me, and even more so, if I survive my confrontation with him, I will lose her. One day I'll be a faint memory, a footnote in her recollection of her PhD process.

I'm terrified she'll forget me. That if I die, no one will remember who I truly was. That the only memories I will live in are those of my father.

"Tell me something about you," Emily requests, pushing a foil-wrapped package in front of me. When I unwrap it to buy time, I unearth a turkey burger. I don't even remember mentioning my preference.

"You seem to already know quite a bit," I hedge, waving the burger between us before taking a bite. So much better than the diner in town, which I'm convinced purchased all its frozen meat in the twentieth century. "What do you want to know?

"Anything," she says. And I think she means it. She's got this look in her eyes like she's apologizing, and I have no idea what for. Maybe it's a projection. Maybe I want to apologize for telling her anything about myself, for forcing her to know me when it will end her.

But I want to. Every day I spend with her, it gets harder and harder to lie and obfuscate. Perhaps this is how everyone feels when they're intimate with someone for the first time. You share your body, and it's natural to share your heart and mind.

It's selfish. But we're past the point of no return anyway. I've already damned her and myself by accepting the extra work and spending so much time with her. Nothing will make this better, so I can make it far, far worse.

"When I was a little girl, my room was decorated like a fairy tale castle. My father used to read them to me before bed, said his mother brought them over from Russia." I have to continue the lie that my father moved to Estonia with my mother, rather than the truthful reverse. There's no point in rectifying it now.

"Did you like them? The fairy tales?" Emily asks, her voice soft and blending with the gentle sounds of the ocean.

"Not really. They were honestly a little frightening, which is pretty standard for Russia." I feel my lips pull into a grimace against my will. "Stories with my father were always about teaching lessons, not soothing me to sleep. He was a very practical man."

"You must miss him."

"Not in the slightest." The words slip out of my mouth without thought, but I can't find it in me to care. He doesn't deserve to be glorified, even in my lies. "He was a hard man, and a lot of things came before me. I was cared for, of course, and I recognize how lucky I was to grow up in comfort. But it came at a cost."

It's the closest I've come to admitting aloud to anyone other than **ДЯДЯ** Mikhail that I know who my father truly was, what he was capable of. That even though I believe he loved my mother, it wasn't enough to stop him from killing her. And that I knew his love for me wouldn't stop me from becoming a victim to the same fate.

If Ilya followed through on this promise—that I was his possession, and he would use and dispose of me how he saw fit —I knew I would find no savior in my father. I would be beholden to my husband's every violent outburst, his demands for sons, his whims for how I looked and walked and acted, and my father would not save me.

"If he were alive, would you try to fix things?" Emily asks, and I finally find the courage to look her in the face. "Would you want him to apologize? Could you imagine a world where he could do anything to make up for it?"

I've never considered it before. I knew my defection was a final decision when I made it, not only because I was ostensibly dead, but also because I know there's no redemption with my father. When I was younger and learning about the weapons trade, I watched him dispatch dozens of traitors. Not with my own eyes, of course. That was too violent for my delicate nature. But I knew what happened to the men he brought before him to grovel and explain their sins. I've made peace with the knowledge that, if I've miscalculated and my father comes for me himself, I'll bite this capsule and swallow every last drop of poison, hoping it's more than my self-imposed immunity can handle. I'd rather die a slow, excruciating death than find out what consequences would come by my father's hand.

Death would be merciful. There are plenty of worse things he could do to me.

"My father's not the kind who makes peace," I answer simply, picking up a chip from the overflowing bag on the blanket. "But even if he was, he's not someone I want forgiveness from."

Another strange look passes over Emily's face, almost like relief. But that's probably also a projection. My hope that, even though I'm not a good person, I won't stoop so low as to beg forgiveness from a man who is incapable of mercy.

"Tell me a story. A fairytale," Emily says, pushing her barely-touched food away and tugging me into her arms. We readjust so she's propped up against one of the smooth boulders dotting the cliffside. I'm tucked against her, my back pressed to the hard muscles and soft curves of her front. Her fingernails rake against my scalp as she brushes through my hair.

A fable appears from the depths of my soul, the way a whale rises from the deep, dark ocean, slowly becoming more and more clear as the light filters through the water.

"Long ago, there lived a family of three—a mother, a father, and a daughter named Vasilya," I start, sinking into the muscle memory of the story, translating the Russian intricacies in my mind. "After years of happiness and peace, the mother fell gravely ill, and knowing that she was going to die, she gifted her daughter a doll."

I hear my father's voice, a ghost of a memory created long before my own mother died. Even now, I can remember her soft laughter in the background as my father took on voices for each of the characters at my request.

I can't recreate them. It's too painful to try.

"*Keep it secret and safe*, her mother instructed. *If anything bad happens, ask the doll for help.*"

Emily's thumb draws circles on my shoulder, lulling me into a trance. I'm not fully here, but I'm not home either. It's cold and windy, even tucked against her body, but some part of my soul is in my childhood bedroom surrounded by stars and spires.

"Years after her mother died, Vasilya's father remarried. But her stepmother was cruel, and came with two spoiled step daughters who never gave her a moment of rest."

"Oh this is La Cenicienta," Emily interrupts, pausing her soothing touch. "Cinderella, in European fairy tales."

"He called it Vasilya the Beautiful," I say. I didn't consume a lot of Western media growing up, and most of my English education was from dated language books. Emily taps my shoulder, which I take as a cue to continue.

"The stepmother and stepsisters demanded Vasilya complete all sorts of chores and tasks, working her until she was exhausted in hopes of turning her ugly. But Vasilya had her doll, and every day she would ask it to complete her tasks, allowing her to rest and only become more and more beautiful.

"One day, Vasilya's father had to leave for a long trip. The stepmother left the three girls with chores to complete and a small fire burning for their only light. But the flame quickly burned out. The two stepsisters demanded that Vasilya travel through the dark woods to...do you know who Baba Yaga is?"

"I've heard the legend," Emily murmurs, sounding like she's also a little lost in a space between here and somewhere else.

"The stepsisters forced her out of their home to seek fire from Baba Yaga. She was more frightened than she'd ever been, but she pulled the doll from her pocket and it soothed her, reminding her she could not be hurt as long as the doll was with her.

"As she continued walking through the night, until she reached the house of Baba Yaga. There were many traps and tricks surrounding the house, but as Vasilya approached, Baba Yaga greeted her. Because Baba Yaga was related to her stepmother, Vasilya had protection against the things that would attack her here."

"Related, that's a twist," Emily says, her chest vibrating with silent laughter when I slap her arm.

"So Baba Yaga brought her into her home and set her a task of picking all the burned grain out of a sack while she slept. During the night, Vasilya asked the doll for help, who called flocks of birds to complete the task on Vasilya's behalf. In the morning, Baba Yaga was angry that she could not punish

Vasilya by eating her, so she set another task of separating peas and poppy seeds in another large sack. As Baba Yaga went outside to tend to her yard, Vasilya again asked the doll for help, who summoned mice to sort the peas and seeds for her.

"Again Baba Yaga was not pleased, so she told her maid to prepare the oven to cook and consume Vasilya in the morning. Once Baba Yaga fell asleep again, Vasilya asked the doll for help one last time, who told her to beg assistance from the maid. In exchange for a silk scarf, the maid gave her the tools to escape the house without setting off the traps. With more direction from her doll, she took a skull from the fence, and its eyes glowed so brightly that it led her home in the dark of the night.

"When she returned, her stepmother and sisters were furious at her extended absence. They took the glowing skull and set it in the house, hoping the light would sustain them for much longer than the flame. But instead, the skull burned down the home, with the stepmother and sisters inside."

"¡Jesucristo! Alice, frightening is an understatement," Emily chuckles, and for some reason that humor is the best reaction she could have had. "At least in the Western European version, the sisters only had their eyes plucked out."

"Still pretty horrifying for a kid's fairy tale," I reply, turning my body so I can snuggle into her. That familiar guilt rolls around in my stomach, shaming me for seeking comfort from her when I know what fate I'm sealing on her behalf.

"Yeah, but in both the Argentine and American versions, the girl ends up marrying a prince."

"Oh, that's how this one ends, too," I amend, picking up the story where I left off. "Vasilya goes to live with an old woman in town and learns to weave fabrics so fine, they were only fit for royalty. The old woman she lives with travels to gift the fabric to a son of the Tsar. But it's too delicate for any of the clothiers to make anything out of, so he asks the old woman to make clothing for him. Vasilya does, and when the old woman returns to give the clothes to the Tsar's son, he demands to meet the maid who created them. When he meets Vasilya, he's so struck by her beauty, that he immediately asks her hand in marriage, and they live happily ever after."

The silence this time is more melancholy, even the wind crying through the trees over the sound of the water crashing into the cliffside. It might only be me, but I think Emily feels it too.

"A happy ending then," she says, but it sounds like a question.

"That's her prize," I respond simply, a vague answer to an unspoken question.

"For being kind? Unlike her stepsisters?"

"For being quiet. For listening to her mother, and not revealing her secrets. And for being useful, I think," I muse, knowing I'm projecting my own pain into this children's story. But I can't help it. Not when I know the lesson my father was trying to teach me. "Vasilya never complained about her chores, and she always listened to her father, even though he brought that pain into her life. She was rewarded for being docile, and that reward was another person choosing her life for her."

Branches creek in the distance. This night is not dark, like the one in Vasilya's journey, even as the sun dips below the horizon. The light of the moon is so bright as it makes its arc across the sky you can see every needle and leaf scattered on the ground around us.

"What would you want your prize to be? For being kind and brave and cunning," Emily asks. My chest pinches with the words she chose for me. Not docile. Not obedient. Not the parts of Vasilya I was raised to embody, groomed to reflect.

"I would want to choose," I say easily, knowing what my answer would be without giving it a second thought. "I would want a lifetime of choices. Of being able to dictate my own life without anyone's influence. No lies, no manipulation, no choices made for me unless I want them to be. The freedom to give up control because I trust someone, not because it's being taken from me."

Emily's holding her breath. I wish I could tell her everything. But she's so *normal*, with her brilliant brain and her research project and her phobias. I can't turn around and say *I'm sorry, I lied, I've faked my death to escape my criminal father and monstrous fiancé, and now I'm becoming a monster so I can kill them before anyone else dies for me, but you might die before I can do that just because you spent time with me, I'm so sorry, please don't leave me.* So I wait for her to say something, anything, so I don't have to.

"I think you're very brave. And I hope you get the life you deserve."

Chapter 12
Emily

"**G**et in the water, you ridiculous child!"

I absolutely will *not* get in the fucking water, thank you very much.

I'm sitting in a much smaller boat than the one we usually use for research. I still have no idea how she convinced me to get on this fucking thing, and I'm finding myself longing for the solid feeling of the Class II under my feet. I am *missing* a *different* boat.

Somehow, Alice is fixing my fear issue. Just not the way she intended to.

But this is a bridge too far. Alice is treading water, her lithe body covered in a thin, pale blue swimsuit that clings to her angles and small curves. She has a pair of comically large goggles on her head, which have a breathing tube attached to the side.

"We're supposed to be doing research," I grumble, pulling my swim cover over myself and crossing my arms. "And anything could be down there."

"Emily, you can see the damn ocean floor from here," Alice scoffs, rolling her eyes as she adjusts the goggles back onto her face. She takes a deep breath and dives beneath the surface, which she's done about a dozen times now, and the world is silent for about one hundred and eighteen seconds before she pops back up on the surface.

"See, I can swim to the bottom and back. It's less than thirty yards."

Somehow, that's not comforting at all.

Alice paddles back over to the glorified raft I'm parked in and grabs the side, hoisting herself up so she's leaning on her stomach, her lower half still in the water.

"You can't be afraid here. You're completely in control," she says serenely, removing her goggles so she can push her hair off her forehead. Her eyelashes are nearly white and covered in dewdrops, reminding me of mermaids and ice princesses and other animated leading ladies.

"I beg to differ," I grunt, looking over the side of the boat with disdain. "Seems like you're the boss here."

I could face this fear, like I do all others. I thought about it when Alice said she had another adventure for me. Like on the cliff and the research boat, I could swallow down the bile creeping up my throat, force my expression to be neutral, and hold my breath until the experience was over.

But after the evening with Alice on the cliff two nights ago, I seem incapable of faking things with her.

She's clearly not working for her father. I've known that she was his victim for a long time, but she's admitted now, in her own way. Between all the surveillance we've done and my personal assessment of her, I can come to Clara with confidence that she doesn't have anything useful to provide about her father or his operations. It's been too long, and there have been too many changes in the past half-decade to assume anything she could tell us from her years with him would still hold water.

I haven't figured out how to convince my cousins not to use her as bait yet. I've been avoiding Clara's request for an update while I try to come up with a plan. But I know I'll figure it out, because I *have* to.

Alice deserves a life. One where she's not hiding from her father, living in fear of his retribution. She deserves truth and honesty and goodness and choices.

And I can't give her those things, not now. Not until we kill Konstantin, and Ilya as well. But until then, I can stop putting on this mask in front of her. I can be afraid, even if that's the only version of myself she gets to see in all it's ugly truth.

"Look at me," Alice says, drawing my attention back to her. She's propped herself up even further now, and bends at the waist over the rim of the boat to grab the extra snorkel she brought.

"You can see everything here, Emily. That's not an exaggeration," she promises, tossing the goggles so quickly that I react on instinct and grab them before they smack me in the face. "Nothing can surprise you. You can get in and out of the water any time you want. The sea floor isn't very deep, so even if you dive you can always make it back up for air. The ocean is calm today, so the waves won't make it hard to swim. The boat is anchored, so it won't drift away. There's a buoy on a line that you can hold on to, so you always know you're attached to the boat and can get back to it quickly." Her expression is hard and serious as she holds my gaze. "You are in control of everything possible here. This isn't about facing your fears. It's about learning that fear isn't necessary."

I still don't exactly believe that. The ocean is so unpredictable...

"A meteor could strike your research lab," she says like she's reading my mind. "Even when you're the most in control you can be, there are still things beyond us."

I groan in defeat, and Alice squeals and claps as I shrug my cover-up off. My swimsuit is of the sporting variety, because temperature-controlled indoor lap pools are more my speed. Even though it's not particularly sexy, I still catch Alice's wandering eyes, which is more motivation to get into the water with her than anything she said.

I pull my hair back into a low ponytail, grateful it's long enough now that the pieces don't spill out anymore, and affix the snorkel kit to my forehead. Alice instructs me to grab the tied buoy and toss it to her, and then I stare off the edge of the boat.

"It's easiest to step up on that little ledge and just jump," she says from about twenty feet away, pointing toward the bench seat that lines the nose of the boat. "If you sit on the rim you might flip the boat."

"Lovely," I mutter under my breath, stepping up onto the ledge. My balance is far less stable here, and I bend my knees and hold my arms out to try to stay upright. Alice's giggles do nothing for my enjoyment of this experience.

"Come on, there's a prize for you if you make it out here," she taunts, swimming a few feet further away. I flicker my eyes up to her momentarily, my blood pumping faster in my veins for a whole new reason. I love when she flirts with me like this. It's only been a few weeks, but her confidence has grown exponentially. It only solidified the acceptance that she wasn't lying. I'm the only person who has ever touched her.

I've never been possessive of partners before, and I know there's something inherently patriarchal and antiquated about the way I feel, but fuck it, I *love* being her one and only.

"Don't threaten me with a good time," I call back, feeling significantly more inspired to jump into the water. I pull the goggles down over my eyes, leaving the mouthpiece of the breathing tube dangling. It takes a few more deep breaths, but finally I conclude that if a giant shark eats me, at least I'll die without ever having to betray Alice.

The water is fucking *cold*. I read the temperature this morning when I was preparing for the day of research, so logically I knew that it was fifty-eight degrees fahrenheit, but fuck does that feel colder than it sounds. My whole body tenses up the moment I hit the water, my muscles contracting in place, and I realize Alice was wrong. I have no control, not even over myself. Panic slams into me like a freight train, and I wonder how long it will take for the mounting carbon dioxide in my lungs to force me to breathe out and inhale pure sea water. I hear drowning is more painful than being burned at the stake, and I have a momentary shred of empathy for all the people I've killed that way.

But then I feel a hand on my arm, and when I glance up, Alice is there. The plastic lens of the goggles makes her eyes seem extra wide, and she smiles in a way that reminds me again of cartoon princesses. When she tugs on my arm again, my blood warms, reminding the rest of my body of its survival instincts. I kick my feet, propelling both of us toward the surface, which really only was about four feet above my head.

"You did it!" Alice screams while I gulp down the air my body was screaming for. Saltwater is in my nose, mouth, and ears, and I shake myself like a wet dog.

"I've never experienced the phrase *frozen in fear* so acutely," I cough out, which only makes Alice laugh more. She helps me grab the line attached to both the fishing boat and the buoy.

"But see, you have control over your body. You swam to the surface, you can breathe. And look below you," she encourages, dipping her face into the water and popping back up, like she's demonstrating the methodology for me. "You can see everything."

When in Rome, I suppose.

When I drop my face under the water, it takes a moment for my eyes to adjust to the strange lens of the goggles. The first thing I notice is our feet, side by side, kicking close to each other. My skin is so tan in comparison to hers, even though I've lost a lot of color on my lower body wearing boots and cargo pants on the research trips. Where I'm all muscle, the planes of my calves tight and bulging slightly with the effort of treading water, Alice is almost dainty. She seems so breakable next to me.

Below us, though, is an entire universe. Kelp grows in a forest thicker than the trees on the cliffs, waving at us in the motion of the current. It's a sea beneath the sea, endless shades of emerald and olive and sage creating its own ecosystem. Small silver and blue fish dart in and out, either on their lonesome or in little schools, appearing and disappearing amongst the leaves.

Alice taps me, and when I look at her she taps the snorkel mouthpiece, which she's placed in her mouth. I follow suit, remembering to blow out first to expel all the water caught in the tube.

We both gaze back down, watching bright flashes of orange, red, and yellow flicker through the maze of leaves. It's like a moving painting, a kaleidoscope of sunset colors and light that my eyes can't fully process.

I pop my head back above the water, my hand still clinging to the buoy line as I blink into the sunlight and remove the gear from my face. Alice doesn't join me, and I watch through the distorted surface as she dives and swims among the seaweed for a few moments.

I know I'm fucked. The options for saving her from the whims of both her father and my family are limited. But now I want more. I don't only want to prove her innocence because of a latent childhood crush, or save her because she deserves a life free from the terror of her father's wrath. I *want* her. More than the imaginary person I created in my head based on a week watching her. This new, real, brave, difficult version of her that I've come to care for.

And I can't have her.

Because even if I miraculously convince Clara not to use her as bait, ensure Ilya doesn't find her, and kill every threat that exists to her, I still have to tell her the truth. That I lied a thousand times over, that I planned to use her the same way everyone who has claimed to love her did, that I am a crucial, integral part of this world she died to escape.

She won't forgive me. I wouldn't, if the roles were reversed. And so even if I save her, I will lose her.

Therefore, fucked.

"You have to come down there with me, I think there's a sleeping turtle on the sea floor," she says excitedly the moment she joins me, a brightness in her eyes I don't think I've ever seen before. "This might be the biggest kelp forest I've found here. There was this big wasting sickness that affected the sunflower sea stars, and that made the urchin population boom, and they have devastated the kelp forests. It's really sad, but this one is amazing, you have to come explore."

I pull her goggles off her face and sling both pairs onto my arm before pulling her against me. Her blush could be explained by the exertion of swimming that deep and holding her breath that long, but I know better.

"I want my prize first," I say, licking the ocean from her skin as I kiss along the line of her jaw. She still hasn't let me kiss her lips, and I still can't figure out why, but I'm going along with it for now.

"So demanding," she replies breathlessly, failing in her attempt at false annoyance. Her hands travel down my back and across my ass, tracing the lines of my swimsuit in a dangerous way.

"Alice..." I warn, kicking harder to keep us both afloat as she focuses on her task. I hoist her a little higher so I can run my mouth over her collarbones, a triumphant glow settling in my chest when I see her nipples harden through the fabric of her swimsuit.

"You always make me feel so good," she says on a slight whine, pushing against my shoulders so I'll let her sink again.

"I love making you come, Pecas," I swear, because it's true. I thought the look on her face, the way her body reacts to my touch, everything about her pleasure might lose its captivating shimmer once I experienced it a dozen or so times, but I've never been so happy to be wrong. If it were reasonable, I'd spend most of my waking hours drawing those sighs and cries from her pretty little mouth.

"But I want to make you feel good too," she demands, her fingers trailing over my breasts, down my stomach, toward the apex of my thighs. My skin flashes hot in the frigid water, and I feel the muscles in my neck tighten with restraint.

Obviously she's touched me plenty in the last dozen or so days, but the focus of our experiences has been her pleasure, which is how I prefer it. Ever the control freak, I like being the one dictating the experience, giving her every ounce of ecstasy her body can withstand. She hasn't made me come with her hands or mouth yet, but I've experienced plenty of orgasms just from watching her take everything I can give her.

That's not to say I'm not interested in shaking things up.

"So eager for me," I praise, grabbing one of her hands and placing it on my shoulder so she's supported by my body. I slip the thin buoy under my other arm so I have additional support as I tread. "Do you want me to tell you how to be a good little prize for me?"

He breaths pick up as she nods, and I lean away from her so she has better access to my body.

Maybe the sharks won't kill me out here, but this might.

"Pull my swimsuit to the side, pretty girl," I direct, thankful that I wore a rather loose one. Alice takes her time, like I hoped she would, dragging her short fingernails over my covered pussy, the sensation both dulled and intensified by the barrier between us.

I don't urge her faster, letting her explore giving like this at her pace. I'll direct her when she needs it, but I want her to feel confident receiving *and* giving.

Eventually she does as I asked, slipping the bottom of the wet fabric aside and securing it between my thigh and pelvis. It's not an easy thing, to keep treading water and be exposed like this, but I still manage to spread my legs a bit more for her.

The water is even colder on my newly-exposed skin, but I barely notice it with the way my blood is on fire. I'm watching her like she's an eclipse, like I can't look away, like it'll burn my eyes to witness but I'm compelled to anyway.

"I want to know what you like," she says softly, barely touching me as hovers her hand over my exposed slit, grazing the short, dark curls there. "Teach me to make you feel like you make me feel."

She really is going to be the death of me.

Chapter 13
Alice

The drive to please Emily, to do for her what she does for me, is almost insatiable. I'm lucky she's so strong, and is ironically a very good swimmer, because she's essentially holding us both up with barely any support from the buoy. Her arms are wide and her long legs kick in smooth, controlled strokes to keep us both afloat. I have a hard time pulling my eyes away from her legs, the contracting muscles of them mesmerizing. I've never met someone so beautiful and capable at the same time.

The emotional turmoil I'm experiencing has become so violent, it's almost like I've become numb to it. My attraction to her, my guilt, my fear, my bloodthirst, my need—it all feels so distant and faint, like the memory of the rolling ocean after you step onto land. I can't seem to come to terms with my feelings, so I'm ignoring them and embracing this. The way she makes me feel, the world of pleasure and *fun* she's introduced me to. I hate myself for damning her, but not enough to stop.

It's the complexity of these emotions, how they overwhelm me, that makes me feel so attached. That has to be the reason. I wouldn't feel so completely consumed by her if I wasn't putting her life at risk. This sensation, like she's the only person in the world I can trust, is because I know she can't trust me. The desire to spend every moment with her, for as long as she'll let me, is because I know both of ours are likely numbered.

It's all too much.

But this? Touching her, being touched by her? Learning, feeling, *living*? That isn't too much at all.

In complete contrast to everything I've ever imagined for my life if I could be free of Ilya and my father, I suddenly want to be controlled. My body and mind both crave being led, being told exactly how to give her pleasure and seeing the way she reacts when I do as I'm told. I want her to dominate me, despite the fact that my most fervent dream is complete freedom from any control.

She's the exception to every rule. Because I trust her, even though she can't trust me.

"Please," I repeat, dragging the pad of my middle finger over her clit, my head swimming pleasantly when she chokes out a groan. "Please tell me what to do."

"Do that again, but a little more pressure," Emily hisses out, her kicking becoming less even as I follow her directions. As much as I love when she overwhelms me with pleasure, this is euphoria of a different brand, equally potent. "Keep going like that, Pecas. Until I tell you to stop."

She drops her head back and seems to soak up the pleasure, and the strange sensation of being both desired and useful fills my chest with pride. I don't know how else to describe it, but it's a relief to know I can make her feel this way, that it's not one-sided.

Her chest rises and falls, quicker and quicker with every second that passes as my fingers rub quick circles. Slowly, so I don't disturb the delicate balance she's created as we float in the ocean, I lean forward and take one of her nipples into my mouth through her swimsuit.

"Fuck, Alice," she gasps, and I feel my core ache with the need in her voice. "Inside me, now."

I hate that I love how demanding she is. I slip my finger inside her and feel her pussy tighten around me, wishing she would demand more of me. Maybe it's because at any moment, I know I could say *jellyfish* and she'd stop without a second thought. I shouldn't have so much faith in her—we've only known each other for a few weeks—but I can feel the truth of it like I can feel my heartbeat.

"Tell me what you need," I say, my mouth still so close to her chest. My tongue instinctively runs along my back molar to check the cap. It's still in place. Which is good, because my body is screaming to do more, give her more.

"You're doing so good," she praises. A combination of pleasure and irritation floods my chest, because I love hearing the words, but she didn't tell me what she wants. I latch my mouth around her nipple again, harder this time, barely pulling with my teeth.

"Jesu—" she starts, only to be cut off when I roll her nipple between my teeth again. "More, Alice. Fuck me like you mean it."

I slip a second finger inside her, pumping in and out, desperate to push her over the edge as she's done for me dozens of times now. The water around us isn't nearly as calm as it was before, but that's not the fault of the currents or the weather. Instead, it's Emily's efforts to keep up floating, less and less controlled with every kick of her legs. Still, she keeps me buoyed well above the surface.

"Give me more, pretty girl. Make me come."

Her eyes are locked on mine as I pull away from her chest and fuck her with three fingers. Testing her strength, I leverage my grip on her shoulder to fuck into her as hard as I can. Her mouth drops open a little, bottom lip so red from biting into it that I almost lose all self control and kiss her. Her eyes flick to my lips too, and it only takes a few more pumps into her pussy to feel her clench around me.

Her muscles flex around my hand, her whole body shuddering as she comes for me, because of me. A broken string of cries and curses in Spanish and a few other languages, if my memory serves me, come streaming from her as she keeps coming. Every cell of my body is on fire as I watch her come apart and stitch herself back together, seemingly forcing herself back down to earth so she can watch as I draw her pleasure out.

She takes in everything, her eyes with their blown out pupils surveying every inch of me. I can feel them on my skin from my lips to my shoulders, to where I'm still pumping my fingers inside her. Like she's trying to capture every detail, creating an image she can keep in her mind forever.

I know I'm projecting. But that's what I want to do. Take a photo in my mind of this moment that I can relive over and over. In my loneliest moments, when I wonder if all I've ever brought to this world is pain and death, I can remember Emily and how she let me be something good for her, even if only for a moment.

"Damn it Alice, what are you doing to me?" she asks, and I can't pretend not to hear the meaning in her words. The desperation I feel too. It's too much, too fast, too impossible, and for all the wrong reasons. But there's no denying the screaming desire to wrap myself in her and never let go.

It's not real. It's my heart's desperate attempt to feel something akin to love before I die. It's not fair, to me but especially to her.

And still, I slip my fingers from her and wrap around her,

so my head rests against her chest and the sound of her heart-beat drowns out all my thoughts.

♡

"You can't plan all the adventures, you know," Emily says, her hand clutching mine as we walk down the only real road in Nesika Beach. We brought the boat back and showered in Emily's motel room—which resulted in a multitude of reciprocal orgasms—before I relayed part two of my plan for the day.

"This is hardly an adventure," I scoff, wrapping my free hand around her bicep and leaning into her shoulder as we walk. "We're just window shopping in the world's most desolate mall."

She leans down and kisses the top of my head, and I realize how much I was really missing as a teenager, even when I learned of my negotiated engagement with Ilya. Every second with Emily feels like I'm floating, like my body is lighter than air. My heartbeat is constantly uneven, and my skin feels prickly with awareness. I crave her attention, her affection, her gentle touch, equally as much as I do her more carnal desires. I never realized that by denying myself something as simple as a crush when I was young, I was missing out on something that felt so good.

All the reasons I have to feel guilty—whether reasonable or not, born from my father's control or my actions—are so much quieter. It's selfish. It's *wrong*.

I smell her cologne, and wonder how long I'll hate myself if I live and she dies.

"Tell me about this place, I've only been to the discount store," she suggests as we walk down the sidewalk, overgrown with weeds and dandelions. The paint of the designated parking spots on the empty street is faded.

"Well, there's a church, two bars, the discount store, a pawn shop, and three vacant buildings on this road," I say, pointing. "The other motel is at the opposite end of the road, but yours is the nicer one."

"A low bar," she mutters, and I poke a blunt fingernail into her ribs.

"Be nice," I scorn. "There's the boat tours and the bait shop by the docks, of course. And there used to be a cheap little gift shop, but the owner didn't come back this summer, so it never reopened."

We walk by one of the empty storefronts, the glass spider-webbed in one of the windows. All of the stores are on the east side of the road; the other side doesn't even have a sidewalk, asphalt transitioning seamlessly into a dirt turnoff, and then grass, and then shrubbery, and then the trees that fill every inch of space until you hit the cliffs.

"I feel like the checkout lady hates me," Emily whispers as we walk by the discount store, Luanne sits on her high stool at the only checkout row, blatantly staring at us through the window. A smile pulls at the corner of my mouth, and I raise my hand to wiggle my fingers at her. She waves back, her brows still knitted in confusion.

"People here aren't great with change," I say, shrugging my shoulders as we meander. "It took me staying through at least a winter before they got used to me."

"Too bad I'm only here for the summer," she says, the end of her sentence trailing like she regrets the words coming out of her mouth. She squeezes my hand, but the air still feels a little more tense as our pace slows.

She thinks she'll only be here for the summer because that's how long her research grant is supporting her. I wonder if she's waiting for me to ask what comes after. If we'll keep in touch. If we'll see each other again.

She could be dead in a few weeks. So could I. And even if we both live, there's no next summer for us. The fantasy that I'll buy a phone just so I can talk to her, the dream that she'd ask me to come with her wherever her research takes her next—none of that is possible. So I keep my mouth shut and squeeze her hand back.

For the first time, I regret my mithridatism. It would likely be easier to let the poison kill Ilya and I at the same time, so I didn't have to live with the guilt, so I didn't have to live in a world without her.

As we walk, I allow myself to imagine a best-case-scenario. Ilya comes, because my father would never deign to leave his stronghold for something as unimportant as his wayward and traitorous daughter. Ilya doesn't kill anyone to get to me, but waits until I'm alone in my apartment. He might even keep me here for a while, to get his revenge for embarrassing him by faking my death before bringing me back to Russia.

I could kill him here. Let him die a slow, painful death from the poison. Find a way to get his body onto one of Jimmy's boats and dump him at sea.

I could live. Emily could live.

But what comes after that? There's no world where my father would let me be. Being a traitor, faking my death, running from him—those are all betrayals he needs to avenge, certainly. But killing his successor? Ensuring he doesn't have anyone to pass the family business to? He would have no choice but to respond, publicly and violently.

I won't pretend I have any hope of surviving my father's retribution, whether it be an execution or imprisonment in his world. I certainly will attempt to take him down with me, but I know the chances are slim. I will die, or find myself back in his clutches with no chance of ever escaping again.

I can't subject Emily to that. I'm already putting her at enough risk, doing it twice would be nothing short of cruel.

If I survive Ilya, I'll go into hiding once more. And Emily might remember me fondly. Maybe the person I really am will live on in her.

"Why does this bar look closed?" Emily's voice jars me out of my silent spiral, and when I look up, we're outside Bait, one of the two bars in town.

"Probably because it is," I say, peering into the dark windows. "Paul owns this place, but he also manages the pawn shop. So he can only bartend after the shop closes."

"There really are no people here, huh?" she replies, the question rhetorical.

"When I got here, there were about four hundred, but most of them are retirees who wanted to get off the grid," I say, remembering what Luanne taught me once she realized I was staying longer than the tourist season. "There are a few people who pick up bartending shifts on weekends, and I think the owner of the pawn shop comes into town from Bend every once in a while, but there are so few patrons it's hard to justify paying people."

"How do two bars stay afloat, then?" she asks as we make our way past an empty and defunct diner, the linoleum peeling from the floor and the formica counters sun-bleached.

"The other one is basically only for locals. Bait serves some basic bar food, so families come to eat there after whale watches, but Wayne's doesn't. Genevieve bartends at Wayne's, she's basically the only person close to our age around here."

"Are you friends?" Emily asks as we pass the lot for the church. I've heard this is a cliche in small American towns. Each one has at least one church and at least two bars.

"Not really, we both keep to ourselves. Last I heard, she's taking online classes, trying to get out of here."

Plus, until I met Emily, I did my best to distance myself from everyone in town. I avoided anything more than casual conversation with everyone I could, hoping it would keep Ilya or my father's eyes off of them.

"You think you could sneak me in? Vouch for me, as a local?" she asks, winking at me as we step over a broken area of sidewalk. The floating feeling is back in full force.

"We'll see," I say noncommittedly, wondering how much I'd regret being hungover on the boat tomorrow morning, and how much I really care.

"The next time you have a day off," she offers, possibly reading my mind, which I find oddly comforting. I'm contemplating something charming to say back when I'm stopped in my tracks in front of the pawn shop windows.

I've been here dozens of times. Paul is surly, and the quality of the food at his bar makes my stomach clench, but he's been a fair negotiator the few times I've purchased things from him. The store is called a pawn shop, but realistically half of it is a thrift store, with piles of clothes in bins labeled *dollar or less* lined along the back walls. That's almost always what I come here for, avoiding the cases of watches and baseball cards and knickknacks, knowing there's no point in buying anything it would be difficult to quickly pack and run with.

But sitting on an acrylic stand in the window is a viola. It's old and a little beat up, the horsehair of the bow frayed and loose in its setting. But all of the strings are there, and the wood still shines like someone once polished it. Cared for it.

I haven't thought about playing in so long. Years before I faked my death and fled my father's home. Once Ilya had a ring on my finger, the golden shackles around my wrists became much tighter. I think he knew about my minor rebellions, about my infrequent episodes of sneaking out of my father's villa and playing music in wine bars and underground clubs. For a while, I turned to more classical pieces, playing in my room or the gardens under the careful watch of my father or Ilya's men.

But soon the experience became bitter. Playing music was about freedom. It was the one small avenue of self-expression I had. Trying to continue when I lacked that autonomy felt like a bird singing in a cage for no one to hear.

I didn't even consider bringing my instrument when I left. I haven't seen one since.

"Are you okay?" Emily asks, and I realize I've dropped her hand. I meet her eyes in the window's reflection, filled with concern for me. Probably because I'm crying.

"Yes, I'm sorry," I say, wiping my tears away hastily. "I...I used to play."

The admission feels strange. Obviously I haven't lied to Emily about everything in my life. But this truth feels bigger. It feels like a piece of my soul.

"Oh," she says simply, her fingertips dragging over the back of my arm. "Do you want to go in and see it?"

I can't. If I do, I'll want to touch it. To play again. And if I do that, I'll want to keep it. And apart from the cost, and the likelihood that it will be left behind when Ilya comes for me, I can't *be* her again.

Other than my need to get my revenge on the men who have hurt me, I have worked very hard to shed everything that defined me as Alisa. The way I talk, think, move. The clothes I wear, the food I eat. Over the past half decade, I've forced myself to not seek comfort in the familiar, so I don't grieve the life I lost.

"Yes," I answer. Even though I shouldn't. Even though I can't. I do.

The little bell rings overhead as we walk in. Paul's head

pops up from where he's reading behind the glass cases, ignoring us once he realizes it's a local and not someone he can upsell to. Emily hovers her hand gently over the small of my back, like she's ready to hold me up if needed. I must look as shell-shocked as I feel.

She's prettier up close. The little knicks on the ribs, the worn finish on the scrolls, all her tiny imperfections making her more perfect. There's no chin rest, no faded spot where one once sat, and I wonder how long it's been since she's been played. This wasn't a display piece, I know that for certain. Someone loved this instrument.

"How long has it been?" Emily asks, her voice so soft it doesn't even startle me.

"Since I was seventeen," I admit, feeling and hearing the shake in my voice as I lift my hand, hovering it over the neck but unwilling to touch it.

"Why did you stop?"

"I was engaged once," I say, physically unable to lie anymore. Not to Emily. Not in front of the instrument that once allowed me to pour all my grief and joy out without saying a word. "He found it childish."

I remember his letter. The list of things that he would not allow in his home, including some of my favorite dresses, the painting from my mother's dressing room that hung above my bed, and my viola, amongst many other beloved items. When I approached my father, he said I should learn to love the things Ilya loved, to be a good wife. That what came into my husband's home, including me, was at discretion.

It was the first moment it occurred to me that I wasn't a person to either of them, but an object. Like a painting or an instrument or a piece of jewelry, I was an accessory. Objects were inherently inanimate, and I was expected to be the same.

I thought my father had loved me as a daughter. But over

the following months and years, I started to realize that all the moments he showed pride in me were those where I was smaller, quieter, *less*. I smiled demurely on his arm, or Ilya's, at a party? Approval. I laughed too loud at a joke? Distaste. I made it through a whole meal only speaking when spoken to? A new dress would appear in my wardrobe the next morning. I asked for leniency, requested independence? Open scorn.

Or in Ilya's case, threats of consequences. Hands on my body. Bruises.

I'm so lost in the memories, staring at the viola like it will transport me back in time if I touch it, that I barely notice Emily leave and return. When she does, she interlaces her fingers with mine.

"You can pick it up," she suggests gently, trying not to spook me. I can't look at her and see the pity in her eyes, so I shake my head.

"I don't want to break it, it looks fragile," I say, a poor excuse. It looks so sturdy, I can almost feel the weight of the wood on my fingertips.

"Break it if you want, it's yours."

My whole body locks, air trapped in my lungs and blood frozen in my veins. Emily's thumb draws smooth, calming circles on my hand.

"No," I say, unable to get more words out.

"I know this is overstepping. And if you really don't want it, I'll take it and hold it until you're ready. But it's clear you once loved this, and you deserve to love it again."

It's too much. There's no oxygen in my body, and I can feel the corners of my vision blur with haze and tears. I might break down, I might pass out. I might stand here for the rest of my life and let the world wither around me.

I wonder if Emily would stand here with me.

"You didn't have to..." I trail off, feeling her shrug beside me. Saying things we don't have the words for.

I lift the hand not attached to Emily and once again try to touch the viola. I don't fear much, but it feels like the moment I touch the strings, a bubble will pop and I'll be back in my father's home, putting my instrument in its case for the last time.

But I do it. I touch the strings, their coiled pattern so familiar and beautifully grating against my skin. The wood of the neck is cold, but it warms quickly. Emily's hand is still around mine, grounding me.

"When you're ready, if you ever are," she whispers next to me as I pick the instrument up by the neck one handed, unwilling to let go of her hand. "I'd like to hear you play, Alice."

Alice. Not Alisa. *Alice*, with the weight of a viola under her palm again. *Alice*, holding hands with someone she chose. *Alice*, being strong and brave, and loving something lost once again.

Chapter 14
Emily

Oh, I am so beyond fucked.

I have no plan. No course of action. Nothing other than the absolute certainty that I cannot sacrifice Alice to her father.

I'm trying to think logically through the panic consuming every moment, but it feels impossible. My family is everything to me. We are strange and harsh and a little cruel compared to the average, but we also love more fiercely than anyone I know. My parents are my constant supporters, always valuing my opinion, encouraging my pursuits outside of The Syndicate, advocating for me with Lucia. My aunts and uncle have never belittled my contributions, even as the youngest Costa. Clara has been my lifelong sparring partner, pushing me to be better, smarter, faster. Our mission has been my guiding light since I could understand the world around me.

And I'm seriously considering giving it up.

It would be difficult. Hiding from The Syndicate would have been near-impossible anyway, but with Deniz by Clara's side, the chances of escaping their oversight are even slimmer. But anything is possible if I'm doing it for her. We could find somewhere new, somewhere by the water so Alice could be reminded of her mother, somewhere where Ilya and Konstantin and Clara couldn't find us.

I could shed everything I am. Permanently become the version Alice knows, constantly working behind the scenes to keep us safe. It would be hard, and painful, and so overwhelmingly sad. But I could do it.

The only other alternative is coming clean and telling Alice the truth. Explaining why I'm here, who I am, how I can protect her from her father. She'd likely balk at the idea of killing him—most normal people don't wish death on others, even the ones who have wronged them. I can't and won't stop Clara, Charlie, and Deniz from getting the revenge they're owed. But if she knew the whole story she might understand.

Maybe I can bring her under the protection of The Syndicate of Fate. Turn her into a witness for us, a fully-informed and consenting one who would have a say in the way her father and fiancé are handled.

Or she might feel too betrayed to consider it. She could try to run, or turn back to her father. And I would have no way to stop Clara from handling the threat to our family and organization.

I imagine Alice's hand hovering over that viola once more, and a sense of grief and protectiveness I've never felt until today floods me again. When I bought that instrument and had one of our Syndicate operatives sell it in this pawn shop, I never thought it would elicit such a reaction from her. I had hoped it might remind her of something that clearly once brought her joy. I thought she might share more with me, not because I need the information for my mission, but because I'm desperate to know her in every way imaginable.

The way she froze. The obvious fear in someone so brave. It

tore me to pieces, more than any lie I've told, or any method I've used to manipulate her.

I was planning to re-buy it for her either way. But after seeing her face, after hearing the agony in the few words she shared, I would have given the world to make sure she knows nothing about her is insignificant or childish. Everything she loves is important.

A pop up reminder dings on my Syndicate phone, informing me that I have five minutes until our meeting, where I need to stare at the only people I've ever loved and decide how much I'm willing to lie. Decide if I can let them go for her.

I push the thought of leaving Alice to fend for herself here out of my mind. Ilya *cannot* touch her. I will not allow it. And I also won't put her in danger of her father's retribution. I have to find a way to make this work.

I have to find a way to keep her.

I take as many deep, calming breaths as I can, waiting until the last possible second to log onto the encrypted meeting platform.

Everyone's already here, and they are all notably silent.

I've been avoiding updating them, and I know they're pissed. Worried too, that I'm failing and this mission will be a fruitless, useless waste of time.

Bea is calling in from her phone, but I can barely see her face with how dark the room is. I have no idea what time zone she's in, much less what country. I hardly ever know what Bea is doing anymore.

Charlie has his arm around Gwen, rubbing his thumb into the crook of her neck like he's working out her tension. Both their faces look wound as tightly as possible, though, and Gwen's sporting a pretty serious bruise under her left eye.

Clara and Deniz are also side by side, but they don't touch.

Deniz's hands are busy navigating a mouse and typing soundlessly on a computer. Clara has her fingers interlaced in front of her. Maybe to resist reaching through the camera and throttling me.

"Meeting is in session," she begins unceremoniously, the irritation from our last family gathering clearly blossoming into something closer to rage. "Updates, Emily."

I imagine Alice sitting next to me like Gwen and Deniz do for their partners. An impossible future, and one I don't even know if I want.

"I believe the best course of action from here forward would be to bring Alice in as an informed witness in our operation against her father."

Clara's lips tighten into a thin line, and I watch Charlie's grip tighten on Gwen's shoulder. Clara didn't ask for recommendations, she asked for an update. But I have to be three steps ahead or everything will fall apart. It likely will anyway, but I have to try.

"I have made progress in learning about her relationship with her father, but I'm unconvinced I'll be able to get specifics about his operations from her without guaranteeing protection," I say, avoiding revealing *how* I came to learn about the emotional distance between them. "Alice believes that any slip-up revealing her past or true identity could bring Ilya or her father to her doorstep. She is incredibly careful, and while she weaves enough truth into her admissions for me to feel confident she has no loyalty to him, she needs to know we can protect her."

"You're advocating for bringing the daughter of the man who tried to kill our Matriarch, who *succeeded* in killing innocents, under our protection?" Clara asks, the question so poisoned with disbelief it sounds almost rhetorical. Deniz flinches, barely. His brother was among the casualties, the collateral damage in Konstantin's attempt to rid the world of his only true enemy.

"If she's to be a useful informant, then yes," I argue, sitting with my hands under my thighs so I don't wring them or pick at my nails and show how nervous I am.

"You personally admitted during our last meeting that her information about Konstantin's operations was likely outdated. You can't have it both ways, Emily. She's either useful as an informant, and we can get that information from her by force, or she's useful as bait."

"I believe those strategies are shortsighted," I say in a measured tone, even though my words are inherently inflammatory. Clara can take criticism, feedback, even an argument when she's in a good mood. Sometimes she encourages it.

She is not in a good mood right now. And I'm not bargaining with my cousin, I'm doing so with The Matriarch.

"Emily..." Charlie warns, but Clara cuts him off with a wave of her hand.

"You accuse me of shortsightedness, but your operation is only one small piece in an endless, intricate arrangement of gears we are moving that you are blissfully unaware of." I bite my lip to keep another argument from slipping off my tongue. "Did you think we would let the reputation of The Syndicate of Fate be determined by your ability to pluck information from this ghost of a girl? What do you think the rest of us have been doing while you've been looking for your sea creatures and mooning over this woman?"

She knows. Maybe not about my history with Alice, but she knows I harbor a soft spot for her. Perhaps it was inevitable. Other than Charlie, I'm the worst at masking my emotions. I attempt to do better now, etching my neutral expression in stone, but it doesn't work.

"You *begged* for this assignment, Emily, and I allowed it

because I thought you might discover an innovative way to bring Konstantin to his knees. I believed you would see reason, that you would eventually understand that, if she was not working for her father and therefore complicit in his crimes and deserving of equal punishment, the best role that Alisa Zakharov can play is drawing her cretin of a father into the light so we can snuff him out."

"So we sentence her to death, then?" I demand, watching even Bea's eyes widen at my outburst. I can't help it, the hypocrisy is too much. "These are the options you've come up with? We abandon this mission now and leave her to whatever sadistic fate Ilya and her father have in store for her. We torture her for information, and have to kill her or dump her, barely alive, on Konstantin's doorstep. Or we use her as bait, and she ends up in his clutches anyway. She is his *victim* and we're willing to sacrifice her for our own vengeance?"

"She could live," Bea says, her voice a near whisper, crackling like she has poor reception. "We could use her as bait and successfully take down Konstantin and Ilya, and she could have a relatively normal life after."

"That's particularly rich, coming from you," I seethe, turning my uncontrollable ire on Bea. "You spend your entire life maintaining the reputation of The Syndicate of Fate as protectors of victims, but Alice is the exception? She's not a victim worth protecting?"

"I don't want to hear another word from you about the reputation of The Syndicate," Clara snaps, her tone cruel and final, more like her mother's than it's ever been. "We are *weak*, Emily. While you isolate yourself and try to save this one woman, every monster we've ever kept from gaining traction sees that we are no longer a threat. They believe that one of the few families willing to match their viciousness to balance the scales of justice can be attacked and nearly destroyed, and there won't be consequences. That we cannot even protect our own, and so why should they fear us? A mission that should have been completely eventless nearly got Guinevere killed, because those who used to cower before us now think they too can light us on fire and we will burn without complaint."

I glance at Gwen and Charlie's screen again and realize there's a bandage on Gwen's shoulder, right where her husband's hand is lying. She doesn't show it on her face, but she must have been terrified. She's capable, and Charlie is an excellent teacher who never would have let her go in unprepared, but she didn't grow up in this life.

"If we forgo our moral compass, the one we will soon pledge our lives and the lives of our future children to uphold, then there is no Syndicate to fear. We are nothing if we sacrifice victims of violence for ourselves," I say, knowing I've stepped far over the line. But this is about more than Alice. Clara is letting fear overcome her sense of duty.

"Enough," she says, her eyes raging like she would kill me if I stood in front of her. She has the right, by Syndicate bylaws, for my insubordination. Treason is not taken lightly in this family. "You will abandon this mission and return home to Bari immediately. We will meet you there to handle this in person."

"I have my research..." I start, ice running through my veins like it's been injected straight into my heart. I cannot abandon Alice. I would rather abdicate here and now.

"If you think your PhD research is a priority for me right now, you have severely miscalculated my disposition," Clara barks, and Deniz finally places his hand on her elbow. It's subtle, and she'll probably eviscerate him for it later, but it does calm the fire in her eyes by a degree.

"And what about Alice?" I ask, feeling bile rise in my throat, working through a thousand options of where we can run in the back of my mind. Trying to remember who owes me favors that they'd be willing to betray Clara for, and knowing that list is very, very short.

"Bea will bring her to Tokyo," she directs. "And from there we'll decide how to dangle her in front of Kons…"

"Wait," I cut in, earning the harshest glare yet. "I'll do it. I'll get Alice to Japan."

The tension between Clara and I feels like standing on the edge of a blade, cutting through us both at the same time.

I know why Clara is doing this. And I hate to admit it, but if it were anyone other than Alice, I might do the same. But sometimes people change us, and denying that is only rejecting the humanity that makes us better than the monsters we fight.

I'm playing my last card and buying myself time. She needs to believe my hysteria stems from my fear of consequences, of losing my place in our organization.

"You have been removed from this mission. You clearly cannot be trusted to independently handle this." She's not wrong. I can't be trusted to do what she wants. But I need to buy myself time to figure out what to do, and if she calls me back to Bari, I'd have to leave now.

"Send someone else to monitor me. Send Bea," I offer, hoping that my shot in the dark is correct. Bea cares about the unintended consequences of The Syndicate's actions. She proved as much at Gwen and Charlie's wedding, when we found out she's been following up with the children of our eliminated enemies for over a decade. I might be able to convince her of my side of this. "I understand I need to prove my loyalty to you, to The Syndicate. We have been confidants since we were girls, and I'm asking you to allow me to finish what I've started. I disagree with your method of handling this, but I'm not the Matriarch, and my fealty is and will always be to our mission. Please, Clara. Let me prove it."

One day I will feel bad for manipulating her like this, for

using our relationship as a bargaining chip. But right now, I don't have time for that kind of moral quandary. Hopefully I can convince Bea that Alice is better used as an ally than bait, and I'll have an opportunity to redeem myself with my closest cousin. But until then, I have to do this.

The family is silent, not a single person breathing as Clara stares me down through the screen. I allow the desperation I feel to bleed through every pore, hoping she reads it as fear of defying her and our family, and not that for Alice's life.

Deniz's fingers squeeze her elbow, so subtly one could mistake it for a glitch in the screen.

"Let me make something perfectly clear," Clara says, her voice measured and more terrifying than it's ever sounded. I've never been on the receiving end of Lucia's wrath, but I know from stories about Gia's stumbles that it isn't a pleasant place to be. I see the apple doesn't fall far from the tree. "If you defy us, if you betray our trust, if you prioritize *anything* over the safety of this family and the continuation of our mission, you will become an enemy of The Syndicate of Fate. Do not delude yourself into believing any of us will show you mercy because of our love for you. Compromising our ability to destroy Konstantin, in any way, shape, or form, will result in your swift and just execution."

She doesn't wait for me to respond. The screen goes black, and the chill that crawls through me solidifies, one blood vessel freezing over at a time.

A few heartbeats later, a text from Bea lights up on my screen. Her flight information. She'll land in Portland in two days, and I imagine she'll drive straight here.

I have two days to figure out how the hell to fix this. And I'm not sure if a thousand days would be enough time.

Chapter 15
Alice

I didn't see Emily today.

She wasn't waiting for me when I got off my whale watching tour. Her car was gone from the motel parking lot when I biked there, and no one answered the door to her room when I knocked.

Which is fine.

Just because we've spent every free second of the last month and change together, doesn't mean she's obligated to continue doing so. It's actually better if she left. She'll probably avoid being collateral damage of my eventual confrontation with Ilya if she leaves now.

I cross my arms on the sticky wooden counter of Wayne's, laying my head down and closing my eyes, like it'll help calm my spinning thoughts. It's not fair for me to be upset. She's not mine, and I'm not hers. There's no future between us, so what exactly am I grieving right now?

I don't even have a phone to call her. This isn't a relationship, it's my last ditch effort to live a life cut short and for Emily it's probably a random summer fling with one of the few age-appropriate people in this tiny town she's stuck in.

"Another one?"

When I pry open my eyes, Genevieve is at the other end of the bar, trying not to look concerned. We're the only ones here, and in the hour since I've arrived I've already consumed three Blackberry Bourbon Smashes, which Gen introduced me to during my first week living here. The idea of a bar this decrepit having fresh blackberry, lime, and mint is ironic to the point of comedy, but Gen loves craft cocktails. I'm pretty sure she picks the blackberries herself.

"Sure," I groan, picking up my glass to suck the watery remnants of drink number three down as she starts making me a fresh one. One would think that consuming rattlesnake venom regularly would make me less susceptible to the effects of heavy drinking, but different toxins affect the body in different ways. I have not created a tolerance for this kind of poison.

Gen doesn't ask me what's wrong, and I'm thankful for it. She's not my friend. Even as a child, I didn't complain and gossip with the few friends I *did* have. Both my parents taught me early on that any information you give someone can be used against you, emotionally or physically. The only people you can fully trust, they told me, were family.

Sometimes I wonder if they isolated me intentionally. If they hoped that making them my only confidants would so drastically narrow my worldview, I wouldn't question the path laid out before me.

I wish I didn't think such terrible things about my mother. She's gone, and I want to preserve the memory of her brushing my hair and singing me songs and taking me to stare at the ocean so I could see where the sirens live. But she married my father, and they loved each other, at least for a significant part of my childhood. She was proud to be the beautiful prize on his arm, and raised me to want the same.

Дядя Mikhail never told me why my father killed my mother, only that he did. And after Ilya's final words to me, I knew better than to question whether it was true or not. Maybe, in the end, she wanted something my father couldn't or wouldn't give her. Or she asked one too many questions, pushed too hard.

The only people I've ever confided in are my parents. They're the only ones who have known my secrets.

Until a month ago.

"There you are."

The relief that floods my nervous system is instantaneous, and I really do hate myself for it. Emily's voice is calm and sure, and I delude myself into believing she's also relieved to see me. I don't pick my head up to look at her, though, mostly because I'm having a little trouble remembering which way is up with the room spinning like this.

She slides onto the stool next to me as Gen places my drink in front of me, and suddenly I have the motivation to sit up straight.

"Where have you been?" she asks, her shoulder knocking against mine. I purposefully stare down at my drink, feeling pathetic and surly and all sorts of complicated emotions that only bourbon will fix.

"Here," I reply curtly, sipping the sweet, smoky drink from the little straws. From the corner of my eye, I see Gen flash four fingers toward Emily. Traitor. I knew she wasn't my friend.

"Why here?" Emily asks, and after a few spinning seconds, there's a glass of water in my hand instead of my rocks glass.

"Why not?"

I know I'm being childish, the thing I hate being accused of most. But all my feelings are tied up and I can't parse them out, can't work my way through them. I keep *feeling* them, and it's fucking awful.

"You weren't at your apartment..." Emily trails off, and I hear a hint of worry in her voice. But I still don't turn to face her, because I'm making a point. What point, I'm not really sure. I'll remember eventually.

"You weren't at your motel," I shrug, spinning the ice cubes in my water with the straw, suddenly realizing I want my drink back. But I'm pretty sure Emily's got it in her hand.

Gen will make me a new one. Where's Gen?

"She's taking a break out back," Emily answers, which means apparently I asked that question out loud. Water is starting to sound like a good idea. "Did you come to my motel earlier? I ran down to Gold Beach to pick up a new battery adapter for the ROV, I must have lost track of time."

Great, now I feel even more pathetic. She was only running errands, and my brain leapt immediately to the worst possible reason for her absence.

Well, second worst. I refused to contemplate the possibility that Ilya had already gotten to her.

"Doesn't matter," I slur, reaching for the glass in her hand and pulling it back to me. She lets it go easily, and I didn't even have to touch her hand to get it. Very proud of myself.

The taste of blackberries and smoke doesn't block out Emily as much as I hoped. I can still feel all her warmness next to me. Smell her cologne, resin and black licorice. Makes me want to taste that instead.

"Hey, look at me," she says, her voice soft and demanding all at once. Why does that make tears well at the corners of my eyes? Why does she make me want to listen?

She drags her thumb against my turned cheek before slipping her fingers into my hair and gently turning my face. When I meet her gaze, she's not nearly as calm and collected as I thought she was. There's a frantic look in her eyes, edging on something that will shred her to pieces.

"I'm sorry if it seemed like I left. I should have called and left a message at the ticket booth." The words are genuine but rushed, like she's trying to force me to hear them before I run away from her. "I wouldn't leave you here."

"Without saying goodbye?"

The words slip from my lips before I can reel them back in. Why would I say that? How could I demand such compassion when I know how this will end? It makes me cruel, perhaps as bad as my father and Ilya, to manipulate her like this. To force this level of intimacy when our closeness may well be her demise.

Emily wipes away tears I can't hold back as she stares into my eyes. She's so pretty. Skin so smooth, lashes so dark, jaw so strong. There are little gold flecks in her irises that I usually only see in the sunlight. But I'm so close to her right now, I can see everything.

"Maybe we..." she stutters, something shifting in her expression. Stronger, more resolute, more desperate. "What if we didn't have to say goodbye?"

Is this heartbreak? I thought I knew what that felt like. When my father told me my mother died. Learning his role in her death. Ilya's words to me that night. I thought those all broke my heart into the pieces that rattle around in my chest now.

But this feels different. Knowing something is just out of reach. Learning something is possible, but not for you. Seeing the thing you want most want you back, and having to deny yourself of it.

"Your research will be done in a few weeks," I say, a weak excuse. I want her to stay, or to take me with her, but I've already knocked over the first domino that will eventually bring Ilya to my doorstep. He will hunt me to the ends of the Earth, because his pride demands it. And I've spent so much time finding a place where the fewest number people possible will get hurt in the ensuing chaos. I can't keep her here, and I can't go with her, bringing more innocent bystanders into the line of fire.

"We haven't found the jellies yet," she argues softly, her voice cracking slightly. "You could come with me, help me find them. You could keep teaching me how to be brave."

My chest constricts, and I realize I'm not really breathing. Not deep enough. She's so beautiful and smart and strong and kind, and I'm going to be the reason she's wiped from the planet.

"I can't go with you," I say, even though I want nothing more than to turn back time and stop myself from making that first call, dropping that first hint to my father's enterprise that I might be alive. I wanted revenge, I wanted to have the chance that one day I might not have to live in fear, or die trying.

Now, I'd give anything to be the invisible woman following Emily around the world.

"Please, Alice," she begs, which only makes things so much worse. So much harder. "I know there are probably things you haven't told me, about why you're here and what happened to you. And there's so much I haven't told you. But we can figure this out. I can protect you."

I laugh. So hard that my belly aches, and more tears fall from my eyes. So many that my tee shirt is dotted with droplets. She can protect me?

"You can't..." I try to say through hyperventilated breaths, but Emily pulls me so I'm tucked under her arm.

"I can, Alice. From anything."

I want her words to be soothing. I want to *believe* them. But they're so patently untrue, and my guilt is morphing into something much more angry. Rageful.

"Why do you think *I'm* the one who needs protecting?" I

nearly yell, liquor churning in my stomach as I push away from her warm embrace. "Because I'm so delicate? So fragile? Big, strong Emily needs to come save me from something she doesn't even understand? Maybe *you're* the one who needs protecting, did you ever think about that?"

The fire in my chest, fueled by alcohol and grief and rage and contrition, grows out of my control. I down the last of my drink quickly, forgoing the straw in favor of getting as much numbing elixir into my system as efficiently as I can. I push off the stool, nearly falling as my feet drop to the floor. Emily's hand steadies me, but I shake her off and start to stalk out of the dark bar, leaving a wad of cash that I don't count on the counter. Gen will tell me if I owe her.

"Alis–Alice, wait," Emily calls after me, and my heart hammers in my chest even harder than before. It was almost as if she…

Her footsteps grow louder behind me as I stumble out of the bar. It's twilight, but the moon is high, giving me enough light to avoid tripping over the cracks and rifts in the sidewalk if I watch my feet very carefully. "There's a lot you don't understand, let me explain…"

"Oh, so I'm both weak *and* stupid now, is that it?" I scream. I don't stop walking, even though I can feel her right behind me. I can't look at her, can't have her see the truth in my eyes. That the thing she needed to protect herself from was me, and I never gave her the chance.

"Pecas, that's not what I meant," she says, her tone begging again. "There's a lot I haven't told you. Please give me the chance to explain."

"No," I reply, the sense of finality I was trying to imbue less intense than I intended. "I don't need your explanation or your protection. I can't leave, and I don't need your protection."

"But you *do*," she insists, bringing my boiling blood to record temperatures. "Please, let me explain."

"Enough," I demand, stopping in my tracks and whipping around toward her, the world spinning with the movement. I close my eyes and take a few deep breaths, trying to will the ground to stabilize beneath me. "I am not this brittle shell of a woman who needs your protection, and I refuse to be treated like I am. If you refuse to accept that, you need to leave."

"Pecas..." she says again, grabbing my elbow.

"Медуза."

Finally, the world is still. The silence surrounding Emily and I is deafening. Leaves skitter on the asphalt, my heart thumps in my chest. But it's all muffled, like I'm under water again.

Медуза. To her ears, *medusa*. Jellyfish, the word we agreed to say if we wanted to stop. Because I needed her to stop.

Except not in English. In Russian.

The words are similar in Russian and Estonian. Медуза versus meduus. Emily doesn't know either language. It shouldn't matter. She shouldn't notice. She shouldn't even know I've said our safe word.

But I see it in her eyes. The recognition of my mistake.

All this time, I was consumed by the lies I told Emily, all the ways I manipulated her. I never once stopped to think that she could be doing the same to me.

There's a lot I haven't told you.

I take a single step back, and Emily stands perfectly still. She doesn't reach out, doesn't try to grab me again.

She wants to. I can see that in her eyes too. But she doesn't.

"Okay, I'm stopping," she says softly, her hands hovering in the air in front of her, frozen in their reach for me.

I should run. She could be anyone. She could be working for my father or Ilya.

The adrenaline rushing through my veins clears the immediate impacts of the alcohol, though I know that won't last long. I have to find a way out of this. I never expected my father to send anyone but Ilya. They're both too prideful to pass this on to a random gun for hire. I've watched both of them kill dozens of traitors and spies with their own hands. Ilya would want to be the exactor of his own revenge.

And he certainly wouldn't have a hired hand spend weeks with me in some elaborate ruse. I'm not that human to him. I'm a cracked gem, a faulty toy, a damaged piece of art. All meant to be thrown away and replaced with something new.

"Do I need protection from you?" I ask. She could lie. She *has* been lying for weeks, and I haven't noticed. There's no way I could know the truth.

"No." She says it like a promise.

I can feel the bourbon swimming to the surface of my mind again, and I try to fight the impact as I take another step backwards. Emily doesn't flinch, doesn't move a centimeter.

Perhaps I'm suicidal. Or the knowledge that I've been living on borrowed time for years has made me value my life less and less every day. But even though I know she's lying to me, somewhere deep within whatever is left of my soul, I'm desperate to believe she won't hurt me.

"I am not fragile," I say, taking two more steps toward my apartment. Not that the locks I've installed could keep her out, if she really was a part of my father's empire.

"I know," she agrees, and she's either being truthful, or this is the most earnest lie she's told.

"I can't trust you." *I want to*, is what I don't say, even though it's true.

"I know," she repeats, this time her expression consumed by regret.

I formulate a drunken plan in my mind, something equally fueled by fear and desire, betrayal and guilt.

"I'm going home, and you are not going to follow me," I direct, and Emily nods her head ever so slightly. "If you want to explain, and you want me to trust whatever you tell me, you'll meet me at the docks tomorrow night at ten. And you will prove to me that you know I am not fragile."

I walk backwards for a few more steps, ensuring Emily stays still before turning and rushing back to my apartment. I don't hear her steps behind me, don't feel her eyes on my skin after I turn up the rough-paved road toward my tiny apartment complex. I secure every lock the moment I get inside, and try to quiet the small voice inside me that reads her compliance as trustworthiness.

Tomorrow morning I might regret this plan. But I can run, if I need to. Hitchhike to northern California, or east into the fields and plains of Idaho. I'll miss the ocean, but now it won't only remind me of my mother. It'll remind me of the woman who taught me to be vulnerable while I taught her to be brave.

And the lies we told along the way.

Chapter 16
Emily

I have less than twenty-four hours until Bea arrives, and absolutely everything has gone to hell.

The sun is setting, the warmth of the day seeping out of my skin as I watch the last rays reflect off the water, spilling like paint. Like colorful ink. Like blood.

Exactly as she requested, I did not follow Alice home last night. I did however spend the entire evening monitoring every camera I've installed across this town to ensure she didn't run.

I don't know what I would have done if she had tried to escape. I wouldn't have had a choice but to go after her. Ironically, it likely would have made my life easier. Clara would get what she wants—a captured enemy and informant—and I wouldn't have to decide if I'm more likely to survive convincing my family to protect Alice, or running from them with her.

But she didn't leave her apartment all day. Even now, so close to our deadline, her door remains firmly locked. I thought about returning her bike, which is still locked up behind Wayne's, but thought she might consider that defying her orders.

I know she thinks I'm working for her father. It was impossible to cover my reaction when she gave her safe word in Russian. For a flickering moment, I considered shrugging it off, asking her if she learned the Spanish version for me, pretending I thought it was Estonian. But Alice is perceptive. I imagine in her father's household reading others quickly was a life or death skill. She knew I knew, and in her world, the reasons I have for knowing are limited and terrifying.

I doubt The Syndicate is even on her radar. Throughout the week I spent with Lucia in Vladivostok, Alice never once joined a true negotiation or business meeting. She was only briefly present at social events where the directions from our hosts were clear—no business talk when pleasure was the goal.

Or at least, that's how Konstantin's generals phrased it.

My only real option is to tell her the truth. Explain my presence here, my family, what her father did, and what our goals are. I can only hope her love for him, and any value for his life, ended as soon as she hit international waters. Because if she so much as hints at warning him of our plans, not even Bea's empathy can save her.

Complicating matters is the understanding that I must let her lead this. She needs to feel strong, in control, capable. She needs to know that I trust her, so she can trust me in return. So whatever she has planned tonight, I have to follow along, and hope it'll pave a path that leads her to listen to my explanation. Quickly.

At nine-fifteen, I watch her front door open, the camera stuck to the telephone pole across from her complex streaming her movements live to my phone. She's wearing jeans and a thin tank top, her hair loose and damp at the ends, like she just got out of the shower. Slung over her shoulder is a tote bag stuffed to the brim. I immediately turn the engine of my rental car on, tapping my fingers on the steering wheel as I watch her move swiftly down the road.

If she was running, she'd have a better plan than simply walking down the highway, right? Though to be fair, hitch-hiking might be her only option. She doesn't have a phone or computer or even internet access in her apartment, so it's not like she searched for bus tickets. She could be planning to catch a ride to the next town with a public library.

I follow her through the cameras as she makes her way past the storefronts we fought in front of last night. I curse myself yet again for the way I reacted. I should have been more in control, should have come in with a better plan. But when I saw her at that bar looking so defeated, and realized it was because she thought I *left*, I couldn't handle it.

It's only been a month. But I've watched her for a lifetime. I've never really left her.

I never will.

She turns down the road lined with a chicken wire fence. West, toward the ocean.

She's coming here.

I turn the engine off, still watching through strategically placed cameras, as I have regularly over the past few weeks. I continue tapping the rhythm of my heartbeat against the steering wheel. The desperate urge to control this moment, to plan everything out, to know what will happen without a shred of doubt, eats at my stomach like a disease. When I step out of the car and into the cool summer evening, I briefly consider changing the plan. Overpowering her, tossing her in the back of the car, and driving off. Trying to convince her that this is for the best, that she's in more danger than she could ever know, that I *will* protect her, even if she thinks she doesn't need it.

But I can't. Not if I intend to keep her.

I have no control here. I have no idea what future the next twenty-four hours will write in stone. Right now, I have to prove to Alice that I trust her, which means facing that fear, swallowing it down, and doing whatever I need to do to save her from all the monsters that hunt her. Including my family.

I close the app on my phone as soon as she turns the corner into the empty harbor parking lot. Her frame is shadowed in the fading sunlight, but somehow even from this distance, I can see the determination in her eyes.

"You're early," she says as soon as she stops in front of me, readjusting the strap on her shoulder. Her expression is stony and unmoving, a harder version of the glassy customer service facade she used to give me, but her fidgeting fingers give away her trepidation.

"I didn't want to make the same mistake twice," I admit. The concession doesn't seem to affect her.

"I have some questions before we begin," she says, breathing evenly through her nose, like she's trying to calm her heart rate. She clenches and releases her jaw. I nod.

"Do you know who my father is?"

There's no more lying. I swallow hard, begging the universe to be on my side.

"Yes," I say, not answering more than I'm asked. I can tell that she needs to drive this conversation, and I want to give her that control, even if it makes my skin itch. Even if I want to try to explain everything all at once.

"Do you work for him?" she asks, her expression tight.

"No, I swear," I reply, wishing I could rip open my chest, certain that the truth of my words would be written on my heart.

"Do you know Ilya Andreeva?"

Know, want to kill, same difference.

"Yes," I admit, wishing I could embellish my response. *I also know Lev, but he's dead and I helped, if that makes you feel better.*

"Do you work for him?"

"No."

She takes another set of deep breaths, probably calculating the probability that I'm lying. If I *were* working for Konstantin's empire, I certainly would be lying. But I also would have had hundreds of opportunities over the past four weeks to take her back to Russia on their behalf, and I hope she's taking that into consideration.

"Are you going to kill me?"

"No." This one I can promise. Even if Bea doesn't end up siding with me, and I can't keep Alice from being a pawn in Clara's scheme, I will not be the one who kills her. Clara can execute us side by side, if she needs to.

"Are you a danger to me?"

I open my mouth to give the same answer, but it catches in my throat. Alice's eyebrow raises, but she doesn't seem afraid, or really even surprised. She looks impatient.

"I am doing my best not to be." It's the most forthright thing I can say without explaining the entire situation, which I don't think Alice wants to hear right now. She nods a little, her expression unchanging, and crosses her arms over her chest.

"I think we're both aware that neither of us has been completely honest over the past few weeks," she says, the faintest Russian accent tinging her words. I wonder if the slip is because she's channeling the cold, distant affect her father is infamous for. "Why should I trust you?"

I had a feeling, if she really did show up to this meeting she planned while inebriated and terrified, she was going to ask this question. And I've been debating all day how to answer it.

I could launch into the full explanation, but it would sound like a preposterous cover. I could confirm all the truths I've told her during our time together, or how she's made me brave, or how I feel about her. But I've decided that Alice has heard pretty words her whole life. But what she wants more than anything else is to know that others have faith in her. That they see her not as a girl hiding from the evils come to haunt her, but as someone who had the bravery to escape.

"Tell me what I can do to prove it to you, and I will. I swear it."

Maybe the universe is on my side, because it seems like that was the answer she was looking for. She reaches into her bag and pulls out a small plastic bag with a tiny triangle inside. In my line of work, unmarked pills in bags are never a good sign.

"Relax, it's motion sickness medication," she says, her voice free of any of the deadpan humor I've come to love. She shakes the little corner into her hand and pops it into her mouth without further fanfare.

"I can't decide if you're a very good liar, or my instincts are very keen. Or I could be losing my mind, who knows?" She shrugs causally as she shoves the plastic bag back in her tote. "But for some reason, I *want* to believe that you're not going to hurt me. So I'm doing something no sane person would. I'm going to let you prove it."

I track her movements as she holds her tote out in front of her and drops it at my feet. It lands with a soft thud, the zipper splitting open a few inches with the force.

"What do you mean?" I ask carefully, watching her blink a little slower.

"You're going to take these keys," she instructs, fishing the familiar pair from her pocket and holding them out to me. "You're going to drive the Class II out to the edge of the shelf. Shallow enough that you can drop anchor. And you're going to break me."

My heart stutters in my chest, and I can feel my eyes go wide. No. This is not happening. This *can't* happen.

"Alice, this is a bad idea..." I start to argue, but trail off when she starts laughing. It's humorless, like last night when I said I could protect her.

"I really don't care," she says, shrugging and popping her hip, a stance I've never seen from her before. Could she be having a breakdown? I can't take advantage of her in this state.

"Are you high? Drunk?" I ask, and she rolls her eyes.

"No, and I suppose you're just going to have to believe me on that one."

"I don't understand," I admit, hoping she's not asking for what I think she's asking for.

"You said you know I'm not fragile," she begins, looking directly in my eyes like the force of her gaze will make me understand. "This is how I want you to prove you're being honest, and that I can trust you in my most vulnerable state. I'll be a little drowsy from the cinnarizine, but I am consenting here and now to have you control my body."

"Alice, there has to be another way," I argue, panic and desire ratcheting up my pulse with equal effect. Of course I've imagined this before, thought about her taking every once of pleasure I have the power to give her, even when it feels like too much. Show her a whole new world of carnality, one driven by experiencing the way every sensation can bring her closer to the edge.

But not now. Not when she's rightfully angry. Not when we haven't talked this through, and I can confirm that she's in the appropriate state to consent to this. Not when I know that fear and ire are motivating her, when compassion and trust should be at the forefront.

"You said you'd do anything to prove I can trust you, and this is what I want," she says with a finality that makes my heart sink and my blood pressure rise. "You can say *jellyfish* any time. Back out. But this is what *I* want."

"I can't," I say, *jellyfish* on the tip of my tongue. I can't give her what she wants. It's wrong. I've lied to her, manipulated her, taken advantage of her trust and vulnerability. I *can't*.

"You can," she says, so much more sure than I'll ever be. "Because I need you to show me that you trust that I'm not breakable, unless I want to be broken. And that I can trust you to only break me in the ways I need."

She's so close, but I don't touch her. Even though I think it's the only thing that will unbreak *me*.

I shouldn't want this, but I do. Not only because dragging her along the edge of pleasure and pain would be the most exquisitely erotic thing I would ever experience. But because I want to show her how closely I can read her body, listen to her words, taste the need on her skin. That we can trust each other in this, and hopefully one day, everything else too.

"I'm afraid," I admit. Her gaze softens the smallest amount, and she reaches out her hands to drag the back of her knuckles over mine. All the hairs on my arm stand on end, and shivers break out across my body.

"Fear isn't necessary," she promises, staring into my eyes like she can see all the way into my soul, search for the dread and excavating it like an artifact, excising it like a tumor. "If I can trust you, and you can trust me, there's no reason to be afraid."

I'M white-knuckling the steering wheel of this fucking boat, repeating her words over and over again in my mind. *Fear isn't necessary.*

This is what she wants. What *I* want. Everything else— her father, my family, the people we are and will always be—

fades away with the shoreline as I make my way further out to sea.

Alice said whatever she took will make her drowsy for an hour or so, and so she's tucked safely away in the small sleeping quarters downstairs. I asked over and over again, confirming a thousand times that this is what she wants. To be vulnerable, to put her safety in my hands, to give all control up to me.

I haven't given up anything, she said as she laid on the cot and shut the door in my face.

I know she's right. I've been a part of these dynamics before, though in a much more structured and, frankly, forthcoming environment. I may be the one driving this boat, choosing where we stop, deciding how she touches me and how she comes, but that doesn't mean I'm in control. The submitting partner can always safe out, can stop the scene any time. Her choice to give up autonomy only amplifies her control of the situation.

That's why these situations are called power *dynamics*. Everything is an exchange.

The problem is, healthy dynamics require communication. Honesty. *Trust*.

It's inherently wrong to use kink as a test of trust. You need to establish it in advance, so everyone feels safe and secure, and knows that their partner has their best interest at heart.

Alice doesn't know that. In her mind, there's a significant chance that I could use this opportunity to truly harm her, or to further manipulate her vulnerability, maybe even at the request of her father or Ilya.

And yet here I am, driving this research boat further out to sea, because she asked me to. Because she told me fear isn't necessary. Because she wants me to prove we can trust each other.

God, this is all so fucked.

The guilt of not telling her who I am claws at me, but I shove it down with the knowledge that if she found out, I'd leave this life for her. I'd abdicate my position in The Syndicate of Fate. I'd kill everyone who has ever hunted her, or hide from them beside her if that's what she'd prefer.

When we're far enough out, I check the radar on my phone to ensure there's no one close enough to hear her scream. Because that's what she wants. To scream, to be afraid, to be used and overwhelmed and drowned in the pleasure of someone else's choosing. To be controlled by someone who will take care of her.

I drop the anchor and make my way around the small boat, taking time to prepare everything. Nylon rope from the spare buoy. Safety shears from the first aid kit. Reminding myself the only thing I know for certain. That Alice isn't afraid. And she needs me to prove that I'm not either.

Chapter 17
Alice

I sit up the moment the engine cuts off.

We're not in the harbor anymore.

The moment Emily agreed to my plan, albeit very reluctantly, I boarded the boat and made my way down to the small quarters beneath the cockpit. The space is barely big enough for a mounted cot beneath a slanted, metal roof, but I climbed into it anyway. The motion sickness medication didn't put me to sleep, but it did make me drowsy enough to lie down and contemplate my decisions.

Emily's right. This is a bad idea. To be honest, it doesn't even make a ton of sense. She could take me out here, do what I asked, and *still* be working for my father or Ilya. This doesn't prove anything.

But for some delusional reason, I believe that this shared vulnerability is the one space we can see through each other's deception. That when she's teaching me to live, and I'm teaching her to be brave, we're the most honest versions of ourselves.

The berth creaks under my weight as I shift, clutching the threadbare blanket covering me and listening to my fluttering heart. My pulse is heavy and cruel, making my skin overheated and sensitive. Beneath the anger, guilt, and shame, there's a steady current of desire. Logic dictates that I should be most concerned with Emily's motivations, and if she is a threat to my safety. But my heart, or some less reasonable organ, wants her to prove that she's the one person who I can trust to both control me and set me free.

I take more deep breaths, not fighting the adrenaline but letting it consume me. I know she's out there, waiting for me. The boat isn't big. Soon enough, she'll have her hands on me...

I have to duck my head when I swing my feet off the bed, feeling the bite of the frame through the thin mattress I was resting on. Metal is cold under my toes, and my exposed skin prickles with goosebumps as I stand. I tossed my tennis shoes under the cot when I laid down, and there's no point in putting them back on.

This is the most reckless thing I've ever done.

And it doesn't scare me one bit.

I climb up the short steps into the cockpit, placing a steadying hand on the railing when a rough wave hits the side of the boat. I didn't expect the sea to be so unruly today, but I didn't exactly check the conditions before I committed to this plan. At least I made sure a storm wasn't coming.

The moon is waning but it's still bright, the crescent hanging in the sky among thousands of stars. The lack of light pollution in this area means you can see the cloud of the Milky Way overhead, stretching across the sky like a beautiful scar.

I don't see Emily, and this boat isn't big enough to really hide on. I pad toward the bow, my bare feet nearly silent against the floor as I step up onto the ledge, putting the railing at waist height. Leaning over the metal bars, I stare into the ink-black water, watching the rippling reflection of the stars above.

It's one endless loop, sea and sky unbroken in their reflection of each other.

I don't hear her coming.

One moment I'm bent at the waist, watching Jupiter's reflection bob on the ocean's surface, and the next her body is behind mine. Her hand is over my mouth instantaneously, muffling the scream that's absorbed by her skin. My heart trips over itself, my instincts demanding I move, fight, get free. But she has me trapped between the railing and her body, warm and strong and soft as she wraps her free arm around my waist, pulling me tightly to her.

It has to mean something that I'm still not afraid.

"Careful, Pecas," she whispers, dragging her mouth and teeth and tongue against the sensitive skin behind my ear. I feel like I'm being warmed from the inside out with her supporting me as I writhe under her grip. "Don't want to fall overboard."

She pushes my upper half further over the railing, her hips pinning mine securely. The hand that was over my mouth is now between my shoulder blades, shoving me toward the darkness of the sea so my ass lifts against her pelvis.

"You want to scream?" she asks, her tone not at all what I was expecting. It's not cruel or demanding, it's gentle, inquisitive, caring. Like we're sitting on this same boat in the middle of the day, and she's asking me about my childhood pets again. "I told you once before, Alice. No one can hear you out here except me. Don't be shy."

I wish I could scream. Instead, a desperate whimper escapes my lips as she slides her free hand up the front of my shirt, palming one of my breasts in her hand.

"What do you say if you want to stop?" She asks, holding her body still, waiting to give me more. I turn my head over my shoulder to witness her watching me, her face almost tinted blue in the moonlight. She doesn't look afraid. She looks like she...

"Медуза," I reply. It's an admission of my deception and hers. Her eyes flash, and quicker than I thought possible, she wraps my hair around her hand and pulls me upright, so I'm pressed against her chest again. I rock against her, this time not in struggle, but chasing the carnal need to be near her, to have her inside me, fucking me, giving and taking everything she wants and needs.

"It's so strange, Pecas," she mutters into my neck, her hand travelling down my stomach to dip under the waistband of my jeans. "The way you pronounce that, it sounds like *medusa*. Do you know what the Spanish word for *jellyfish* is?"

Even if I had the capacity for conscious thought, I wouldn't know what to say. She's telling me I could have lied. There was a believable excuse for my slip up, and I didn't even know it existed.

One-handed, she undoes the button of my jeans and drags the zipper down.

"Such a coincidence, the tongues of our father's homelands would share this word."

She slides her hand beneath my underwear, dragging her fingers against my clit and to my entrance. I'm absolutely soaked, evidenced by the lewd noises created when she cups my pussy and barely presses her middle finger inside me.

She's using our lies and deception to fuel the tension between us, to feed this lust and need, and it's working.

"So wet for me, pretty girl," she murmurs, pulling my hair even harder so my head snaps back against her shoulder as she fucks me deeper.

It's already too much. The feeling of her body against mine, supporting me while I melt around her like wax near a flame.

Her ragged breaths as she gets turned on just by touching me. The way she presses the heel of her hand against my clit each time she pumps into me.

"I'm gonna…" I choke out, the words cutting off as she fucks me faster, forcing me closer and closer to the edge of my orgasm.

"Over and over, Pecas," she swears, her teeth nipping at the skin of my neck. "I'm going to teach you all the ways your body wants to be used. And I won't stop until you physically can't take any more, and maybe not even then. Now come for me."

Like her command was all I needed, the orgasm rips through me, my pussy clenching on her fingers as every muscle in my body contracts. I don't muffle my cries, letting the darkness surrounding us consume every wave of pleasure.

The orgasm hasn't even completely ebbed before she pulls her fingers out of me and holds them to my lips.

"Open."

For a moment I hesitate, the euphoria clearing and self-doubt stirring. When I don't respond quickly enough, she grips my chin and forces my mouth open.

"Just like that," she praises tenderly, even though I didn't do what she asked. She pauses, giving me a minute to safe out, but that is the absolute last thing on my mind. Before I met Emily, I could probably count on one hand the number of times I had recognized that I was turned on. But even including all the times since she started teaching me what it feels like to want and be wanted, nothing has been so explicitly erotic as taking her fingers into my mouth and tasting my own pleasure on her skin.

When her fingers are clean, and her pupils are blown to the size of saucers, Emily manipulates my body so my back is against the railing. And I let her, because it feels so good to have her hands on me, to be able to trust her, even though I shouldn't.

"On the floor," she commands, and my body follows her direction with ease. I preen internally when she smiles as my ass hits the ground, my jeans shucked low across my hips so the metal of the railing bites coldly into my lower back.

All the soft afterglow, the hazy post-orgasmic peace, disappears immediately when she pulls a length of rope from where it's tucked into the back of her pants.

"Emily..." I say cautiously as she kneels in front of me, brushing my hair behind my ears so she can see my face.

"I need you restrained, Pecas," she coos, taking one of my hands in hers and gently stroking my wrist, right where I can imagine that rope. "So you can't pull away when I show you how good I can make you feel."

It feels impossible to be this turned on again, but my nipples are tight and sensitive against the fabric of my tank top, and all the remnants of drowsiness from the medication are gone. Emily wraps the rope in loose, intricate loops around my wrist, the nylon tightening against my skin when she pulls my arm up over my head.

"Relax your arms, and it will loosen," she instructs, looking down and winking at me as she ties the other end of the rope to the top bar of the railing. Looking this sexy while having complete control over my body should be a criminal offense. "Pull against it, and it will tighten."

"Is it dangerous?" I ask, my question earnest even though my tone is soaked in lust. Emily slips her hand into her back pocket and pulls out what look like medical shears.

"Yes, any bondage is dangerous," she replies, the explanation slightly more clinical, but still making my need grow stronger. "But if you feel painful tingling or your hands get cold, use your safe word and I'll cut you free."

Someone I couldn't trust wouldn't say this. A contract kidnapper or killer wouldn't make me feel this safe, this cared for, this *loved*.

Right?

By the time she has both my hands tied over my head, I still don't have the answer. But the hunger in her eyes erases any other thought than *please* from my mind.

"Now for the fun part," she says with a smile that could kill me.

From her apparently boundless back pocket, she produces a thin, black object that I can't see clearly in the limited light. That is, until she clicks a small button, and silver flashes in front of me.

My heart jumps into my throat. Every inch of my body is frozen, even the blood pumping through my veins. This could be it, and it would without a doubt be my fault. I run my tongue over the cap on my molar, feeling for the loose spot that I can easily dislodge. The capsule hidden in the back of my mouth is my last resort, if I have made a grave mistake. This amount of poison wouldn't kill her immediately, but hopefully it would make her sick enough to distract her while I freed myself.

I can use the stars to swim back to shore. It's not ideal, and being in the ocean at night with little visibility isn't something I'd recommend, but I would have a better chance at surviving the open water than on the boat with someone so much stronger than me.

Even now, I don't feel afraid.

There must be something wrong with me. But as the knife glints in Emily's hand, reflecting the moonlight pouring over us, I feel it in my bones. She won't hurt me.

Still, it's good to have a backup plan in case I've lost my mind.

Emily holds the blade closer to me, and my heart rate picks up another notch. I shouldn't be turned on. I've seen first hand what a simple fishing knife can do in the hands of someone adept and skilled. And clearly, with the way she rotates the hilt between her fingers, Emily is. But there's no denying the slickness between my legs as she catches the collar of my tank top on the tip of the blade.

"I promise, I'll buy you three to replace it."

She drags the blade downward, pulling away from my body as she goes and splitting the fabric of my top in two. The sea air hits my overheated skin, spreading goosebumps across my flesh like wildfire. With a few more simple cuts, she's reduced the shirt to shreds of fabric, and I'm bare from the waist up. Emily resheathes the blade and returns it to her pocket, all the while tracing every inch of my exposed flesh with her gaze.

"I want to see all of you," she says, not like a request but like a warning. With my arms above my head, I can't help or stop her as she pulls my jeans and underwear down my legs.

Emily repositions herself so she's on her knees on the floor of the boat. With me sitting on the higher ledge, it puts her in the perfect position to devour any part of my body she wants. I close my thighs, not because I don't want her to see what she's tasted a dozen times before, but in an effort to relieve a fraction of the pressure already building in my core.

"None of that," she admonishes, and I can't stop the whine that escapes from my lips as she pushes my thighs open, the cold bringing a sharp edge to the mounting pleasure.

"I love seeing you like this." Emily's voice feels distant, like she's in another world, as I feel her drag the tips of her fingers up the back of my thigh. My muscles tense, my hips rolling forward to meet her hand, but she pulls away right before she touches me where I need her.

"Please," I hear myself beg, tilting my head back against the bars and pulling against my restraints, savoring the feeling of the soft rope biting into my skin.

"What do you want, Pecas?" she asks, the nickname rolling off her tongue like syrup. She told me what it meant the day she first used it. *Freckles*, she explained as she drug her tongue across the constellation on my shoulder.

"It's too much," I repeat, my skin so sensitive it feels like I'm on fire. Especially where she touches me, on my thighs, my ankles, my hips.

"And that's what you need. Too much." As if to emphasize her point, she digs her nails into the skin of my hip, leaving marks above my ass. "Isn't that right?"

"I need whatever you give me," I plead, meaning every word. I need her to be in control, to be allowed to lose my grip on reality and know she's there to hold me up and bring me back when the time comes.

"Such a good answer from such a good girl," she praises, my behavior earning me a gentle circle of her fingers over my clit. I'm still flushed from my first orgasm, slightly overstimulated, but it feels so good I can't find it in me to care. She pauses for a moment, watching the way my hips roll against her fingers, chasing more.

Without another word, she grabs the back of her tee shirt and pulls it over her head, leaving her in a tight-fitting, low-cut sports bra that makes me want to be the one tracing her skin with my tongue. She taps my hip, and confused but obedient, I leverage myself to lift them as she slides the shirt underneath.

"Didn't want to hurt that perfect ass," she says, grinning when I use it to slide closer to her, so I'm perched right at the edge of the ledge. "Well, not that way."

The thought of her hand marks on my ass drives another

wave of lust through my body, and I wonder how much I'll have to beg for her to touch me again.

"Emily, I need you," I admit, shivering as she pulls one of my nipples between her fingers and rolls gently.

"I know." A pinch, this time harder. I pull on my restraints as a cry out again, feeling my empty pussy clench. "And what if I want to fuck you rough? Make you soak my hand and come until you cry? And once you're satiated and overstimulated, put you on your knees in front of me so you can say thank you?"

I nod a thousand times, hoping her threats are promises.

Two fingers slip into my entrance almost immediately, coupled with the feeling of her mouth on my nipple. She isn't gentle, teeth scraping against the sensitive skin as she fucks me at a ruthless pace. Two fingers become three as she crooks them upward, stimulating a place within me even she hasn't touched before.

Everything feels shaky, like I've touched the third rail and every molecule has become electrified. There isn't enough air in my lungs, and my vision hazes at the edges as a new kind of pleasure settles deep in my bones. The pressure in my lower abdomen intensifies a hundred fold, and I pull harder against the ropes to feel the bite, to let it ground me when I feel like I'm floating above my body.

"Emily, it's...I..."

She doesn't stop. Doesn't slow, let up, give me any semblance of relief. I'm climbing to a peak I've never reached, different from the ones she's brought me to before, and I know it's going to shatter me to fall off the edge.

And shatter I do. The pressure releases, and I soak her hand, just like she told me I would. She doesn't stop, moaning her approval as she continues to dole pleasure to my breasts and pump ruthlessly into my pussy. I feel like the orgasm will never end, a freefall of epic proportions that leaves me struggling for words, for thoughts, for air. I close my eyes and swim in the feeling, crying out into the night a string of words that are mostly her name.

Finally, *finally*, when my body slumps against the railing and my bones feel liquified, she stops.

For a few moments.

My eyes snap open when I feel her hot mouth on my pussy, her tongue dragging from entrance to clit. She closes her mouth over the bud and sucks, and I really scream this time. The pleasure of her mouth is buried under overstimulation and pain, but somehow it's still *good*, and I'm not sure how that's possible.

"You make such a pretty mess for me, Pecas," she says, licking her way up my pussy again. Her words, the groans of pleasure, the way she grinds her hips against the side of the ledge to get some relief—it all makes the pain worth it.

"I can't again," I say, not sure if I mean it or not. But she doesn't seem worried, sucking on my clit again. "Please Emily, it's too much."

"I don't care that you think you can't," she replies, her fingers replacing her lips as she circles me, her spit and my cum creating a slick surface for her work. I close my eyes against the discomfort, focusing on the ecstasy beneath. "You said you wanted to take what I can give you, and I'm going to make you keep your promise. I need you to come on my mouth before I use yours."

Черт, I want to do that so badly, it pushes my body deeper into the pleasure. I know it'll take much longer this time, but Emily doesn't seem to mind the work. She doesn't touch herself, but her moans tell me she's enjoying herself as she lets me grind my clit against her tongue, forcing myself closer and closer to yet another release.

It's more drawn out this time, the orgasm starting in my toes and spreading throughout my body like it's infecting me, cell by cell. My back arches, lifting my hips off the tee shirt-covered deck and harder against her mouth. My throat hurts, and I realize it's from crying out her name as I let this pleasure consume me, drown me, pull me into depths far more terrifying than the ocean below us.

I'm gone from this mortal plane, my soul hovering above my body like it'll distance me from the Earth-shattering feeling I just experienced. I groan as Emily undoes the rope holding up my arms, massaging my sore wrists and shoulders.

But the night isn't over.

Emily bears most of my weight as she walks us to the cockpit and settles me on my knees in front of one of the benches. My head still feels floaty and distant, but I'm conscious enough to watch Emily disrobe, tossing her boots and socks, work pants and underwear and sports bra, into a distant corner before sitting in front of me on the bench.

I'm mesmerized by her body. Lean and muscular, soft and forgiving, all at the same time. She contains everything in one frame, surpassing my previous understanding of *beautiful.*

She angles her body so her ass is on the edge of the seat, similar to how I was positioned a few minutes ago. The movement exposes her pussy to me, just as wet as I was too.

She may seem nonchalant and unaffected while I'm writhing beneath her, but this is evidence enough that she needs me exactly as much as I need her.

"Show me how you say thank you."

I don't need further invitation.

Instantly, I'm buried against her, copying the motions she performed on me in a desperate attempt to please her. Her fingers lace into my hair, pulling so hard it makes me cry out against her. She maneuvers me to exactly where she wants me, barely moving her hips, wordlessly telling me that I'll have to work to show her how grateful I am.

"Two taps on my thigh if it's too much," she says, demonstrating with her free hand. "But you won't need it, will you, pretty girl? You love being used by me."

I do, I say inside my head, sucking harder on her clit instead of voicing my assent. She keeps my face pressed close to her with her hand in my hair, and I angle my chin so I can press two fingers inside her.

"That's it, Pecas. Be exactly what I need."

Fucking her like this is otherworldly. She tastes so good I could spend days on my knees in front of her, letting her fuck me and use me to come however she wants. I wish it would take hours. I want to be here all night, feeling her clench around me as I work her toward a fraction of the pleasure she provided me with.

Emily comes, praising me with every word that comes out of her mouth as she rides out the orgasm *I gave her*. Taking cue from her, I don't let up, licking and sucking and pumping into her until she physically pulls my face away from her body. My lips and chin are covered in her wetness, and she pulls me up toward her, leaning down so we're mere centimeters apart.

"Use your safe word," she demands, her lip barely brushing mine, the ghost of my pleasure on her mouth. I feel for the cap with my tongue, relieved to find it unbroken.

Because I want this too.

"No," I say, relishing the feeling of her grip tightening in my hair.

"So fucking difficult," she sighs, and then her lips collide with mine.

I didn't think, after everything we'd done—the touching, the lying, the fucking, the vulnerability—that kissing her would be the thing that pushed me over the edge of trusting her. But her tongue is in my mouth, and we taste like each other, and I know beyond a shadow of a doubt that she's the only person in the world I can actually trust. She cut my restraints free. She embraced me in my vulnerable state and gave me everything I needed and more.

And no matter what she's been hiding, I know she was right. She will protect me.

And I'll find a way to protect her.

Chapter 18
Emily

I have to tell her.

It's unhinged, but I've known Alice—*Alisa*—would be mine since the moment I saw her on that stage.

I love my family, especially my parents, with every fiber of my being. They've been supportive, accepting, and my greatest champions since the moment I was born. But we are who we are, and softness has never been an option between us. With them, love is something that is patient yet demanding. It makes you vulnerable, so therefore it must also make you strong. It's the knowledge that your family will choose the mission over you, every time, because they know you'll do the same, for the greater good.

But as I carry Alice back to the cramped cot beneath the cockpit, her cheek pressed against my chest and her eyes fluttering closed, I know this type of love is different. I cannot imagine a world where I don't choose her. If given the option between the work of The Syndicate of Fate and her, I wouldn't hesitate. If she demanded I kill her father, I'd do it, consequences for The Syndicate be damned. If she asked me to burn the whole damn world down, I'd do that, too.

If she asked me to leave The Syndicate…

Grief tightens my stomach as I lean over to lay her on the berth, her hand still clinging to the collar of my shirt.

I would. I would leave my family and this work I believe in, if it would make her happy. And it would be excruciating, not to have Clara and Charlie and Bea in my life, to never see my parents again, to be unable to help avenge Zia Lucia. There would be a part of me that ached for the purpose they gave me, the love we shared. It wouldn't just be losing them, it would be *running* from the people who love me most.

But that pain pales in comparison to the idea of losing her.

I gently peel her fingers off my shirt so I can re-dress her in the sweatpants and tank top she packed in her bag. It'll be warm enough under the blanket with her body pressed to mine, but I don't want her to freeze if she gets up in the middle of the night.

She's too exhausted to be much help, but we eventually get her clothed and I slip onto the thin cot next to her. Her face is immediately in the crook of my neck, her arm around my torso, and I pull her as far on top of me as I can. I need to smell her sea salt and blackberry hair, and to feel the warmth of her skin, and to buffer her against the rather uncomfortable berth frame.

It's only a few minutes before she's fully asleep, and while exhaustion threatens to pull me under as well, I can't help my spiraling thoughts. There has to be a way to explain to her who I am, why I'm here, why none of that matters anymore. We both know we can't continue lying, can't keep up the stories we've been spinning. Beginning this life with her means coming clean and starting fresh. I have to allow her a choice— she's been given so few in her life, and I won't be another person who denies her freedom.

She's entitled to the truth, even if it makes her hate me for a while. I deserve that. But if she cares about me a fraction of the amount I love her, we will be able to work through it.

Tomorrow. I'll sit her down and explain to her who I am and why I came here. I'll answer every question, give her all the time she needs to process.

But after tomorrow, Alice will have no doubt that she is the most important thing in the world to me. That's the thought that comforts me as I drift off with the gentle rise and fall of our boat on the water.

I'M A MOMENT TOO LATE.

Just a second too slow.

I wake up a single heartbeat before I feel a pinprick in my neck. The adrenaline of fear barely has time to course through my system before it's sedated by whatever's being pumped through my veins.

With the dying remnants of my strength, I hold Alice to my chest. I can feel something pulling her away, a darkness I can't perceive. Like the unforgiving gravity and incessant pressure of the deep, the figure drags her away from me, and I dig my nails into her skin in a futile attempt to keep her here.

I knew I should be afraid of the sea, I think, my mouth too filled with something that tastes like copper, like blood, to speak the words aloud. *I knew it would take something from me. Why is it taking her? She loves the ocean so much. Why is it being cruel to her?*

Her weight lifts from me, my grasping fingers failing me at last, and a vision of gold and red and orange filters through my memory. And I hear it, the sound of a horsehair bow pulled over delicate strings, so clearly that she must be playing for me.

I was right. All those years ago, I was right.

The sounds of Alisa Zakharov are what will lull me to the other side.

What a beautiful way to die.

Chapter 19
Alice

What a fucking bitch.

I'm so goddamn mad at myself, I can't even feel the heartbreak I know is lingering beneath the rage. Rope much less forgiving than the one that bound my wrists a few hours ago scratches at my skin, wearing away at it until I bleed every time I move. My whole body screams with a horribly lethargic pain. It feels like I can't contract my muscles, like I don't have the strength or capacity to will my body into motion. At the same time, I know doing so would expel the sensation that wasps are making vicious homes in my joints.

I *hate* her.

I hate myself for trusting a gut instinct that has done nothing but lead me astray. I hate that she made me vulnerable and open and *myself*, only to rip that away after I'd given her everything. I hate that I handed over every ounce of control, and instead of cherishing it like I trusted her to, she took and took and took until I had nothing left to give.

I try to think past the excruciating physical and mental anguish to assess my situation. I'm definitely on land—I would recognize the feeling of even the calmest seas beneath me. I'm tied to a metal chair, and I think I've been here for a while, considering the metal is warm from my body heat. Everything is sore but warm, so we must be somewhere climate-controlled, or it may be daytime. There are no windows, no light, nothing surrounding me except the concrete floor beneath my feet. I have no idea how long I've been out.

There's an acute pain in my left shoulder. I assume that's where Emily injected me with some sort of paralytic, which must be synthetic because my body doesn't seem to have a tolerance for it. I instinctively run my tongue over the cap at the back of my mouth, relieved when I find it intact. I suppose I'll have to decide if I need to use it on her or wait until she turns me over to Ilya.

I try not to think about the way I'll have to press my lips to hers again to pass the venom into her mouth. I had accepted I'd have to kiss Ilya to kill him, I can do it with Emily too.

Even if it feels so much worse to bear.

I take deep breaths through my nose, trying to fight the familiar nausea clutching at my stomach. I need whatever's in my stomach to stay put, mostly to avoid dehydration. I have no idea how long I'll be down here until Ilya or Emily or my father comes to retrieve me, and I must conserve my strength.

I truly do not know what I'll do if Konstantin Zakharov is the evil I face today. My entire plan has hinged on Ilya wanting revenge on his traitorous wife, and my father being too proud to chase after an errant child. If I'm wrong, I have no strategy to kill my father. Passing the venom to him from my mouth is obviously out of the question, and unfortunately by design there isn't enough in this capsule to kill myself before he can bring me back to Vladivostok.

I hadn't planned past Ilya, because I wasn't sure I'd survive him. I'm regretting that now.

In the distance, a heavy door creaks open. No light filters

in, so the entrance to this place must be far from me. My heart beats faster and faster, fear overriding the effects of the drugs in my system as I try to focus my adrenaline on categorizing what I hear. Footsteps, one pair. Heavy, slow, coming from behind me and to my right. They're not Emily's, unless she's purposefully changed her gate. I have the sound of her walking from her motel bed to the kitchenette sink to get me water burned into my mind. I'd know if it was her.

I'm reminded of my failure when a tiny thread of disappointment snakes its way into my heart, constricting around it like a thin, deadly tourniquet. I am *disappointed* that I won't see her. That I might never see her again, now that she's completed her job.

So fucking pathetic I could scream if it wouldn't make me puke.

What feels like an eternity later, the footsteps grow loud enough that I know they're close. They stop behind me, and they don't smell like anything. Not perfume or aftershave, not gunpowder or the sea or black licorice.

Which tells me exactly who it is.

"Hello, Ilya."

A small click, and yellow, fluorescent light from a swinging overhead bulb floods the area directly around me. The concrete beneath my feet is stained—maybe with oil, maybe with blood. With a flare for dramatism I associate with his brother, Ilya walks around me slowly, seeing if I'll turn my head, if I'll flinch first.

I want to keep facing forward, refuse to show him fear. But I know that for my plan to work, he has to think I'd do anything to avoid being killed. So I whip my head over my shoulder, curving my posture in like I'm afraid he'll strike me.

Not a wholly unreasonable fear, knowing how our last interaction ended.

"Alisa," he says, voice devoid of any emotion. I didn't really expect much, but irritation and rage were possibilities. Should have known better. "You look well, for a dead girl."

I dart my eyes away from his cold glare, letting unfamiliar, manufactured fear flood me like a tide. I'm certain he can smell it, that he likes it.

"Where am I?" I ask, even though I'm fairly certain I know. There's a defunct shellfish processing warehouse about thirty miles inland from the harbor. Ilya is a creature of habit, ruthless yet predictable. On the few occasions I was privy to his actions, he either brought victims back to Vladivostok so he had complete control over his environment, or he stayed as close to the abduction site as possible. *Travel is the most vulnerable function of an operation*, my father once told me, in one of the rare moments he shared his work with me. I'm sure he taught Ilya the same.

My muscles would be stiffer if I had been out long enough to get all the way back to Russia.

"That is not what you should be concerned about," he replies, his hands in his pockets so casually, like this whole situation is no more than an irritating errand.

"Ilya, I'm sorry, please don't—" I start, feeling false tears prick at the corners of my eyes. I was worried my acting wouldn't be convincing, but so far I'm doing a pretty good job, if I say so myself.

"Your death was inconvenient, Alisa," he says, speaking over me. I clamp my mouth shut, annoyance cutting through my fabricated fear before I shove it back down. "Our union made the succession of your father's empire easy, smooth. No one would dare challenge his decision to pass the torch if I was his son-in-law. But with you dead, I've had to maintain a very delicate balance to ensure I stay in his good graces."

He squats in front of me, resting his forearms on his knees

and staring into my eyes. There's a new-to-me burn scar on his hand, covering most of his pinky and ring finger and traveling past his wrist. His hair is so short now it's barely a shadow on his pale head. But those pale green eyes are the same. Cold and distant and assessing. Critical and disengaged.

Cruel.

"Your absence opened the door for him to consider others. He thought merging with another enterprise might expand our network. Not only guns, but drugs. People. Information." I fight the roiling in my stomach at Ilya's words. I wonder, if I had gotten what I wanted as a teenager, would I have ever balked against my father's operations, his evil greed? I hate that I don't know the answer. "So you see, my wife, you should not be concerned about where you are. Your only question should be *how can I fix this, my husband.*"

"I don't—I thought you'd kill me if you ever found me," I reply, honestly surprised that he's presenting me with the option *to* redeem myself in his eyes. My father always seemed so fond of him, I never imagined a world where my marriage to Ilya would be his anchor to our power. And even with that being the case, I'm shocked Ilya's pride would allow him to take me back, no matter the conditions.

"I may still," he replies, still emotionless, like my life means less than nothing to him. "But you could be more worthwhile to me alive. If I bring you home, Konstantin will be so grateful he will find me in favor again. And with our engagement still intact, perhaps he'll have no choice but to name me his successor."

Ilya stands back up, a rueful smile pulling at the corner of his mouth when I flinch at his movement. He must be as desperate as I am, because his plan is fundamentally flawed.

"My father would never let a traitor back in his stronghold," I say, knowing the truth of it deep in my bones. He's killed dozens, if not hundreds, for much lesser crimes. My mother, a woman I believed he once truly loved, likely died because he no longer wanted to tolerate her discontent. Being his daughter would not save me that wrath.

"A traitor?" Ilya asks, patronization soaking his tone. "What a horrible misunderstanding. No, Alisa Zakharov was kidnapped by her uncle, who began working for one of our enemies when his sister tragically drowned. She was a victim of one of the families who dares challenge us. But I found her, and she is *ever* so grateful to be home."

He *is* desperate. I may have been obedient, but it's not like I kept my growing discontent a secret from my father, especially where Ilya is concerned. And even if I played along with his story, my father is paranoid enough to demand evidence of its veracity. We have many enemies, but it wouldn't make sense for one of them to kidnap me for half a decade and not use it against him.

"He's never going to believe that," I say, trying to make my tone less argumentative and more despondent. He's already taught me what fighting with him will earn me, and I don't want another permanent mark from him on my body, the scars on my hip already too many. If I seem desperate, he'll feel in control, and that's where I need him right now.

"He will. Because you're going to convince him," Ilya responds, brokering no argument. He pulls a switchblade from his back pocket, the movement so similar to Emily's that I feel a pit open up in my stomach. But this time, I *am* afraid. He is out of his mind, and every word I speak pulls tighter on the tripwire of his desperation. "You will be bruised and bloodied, have a few new scars, of course." Ilya flips the handle so the tip of the knife is pointing directly at my heart. "But you will sob at his feet and tell him how grateful you are, how horrid your captors were, how you *need* a hastened wedding to thank your ever-dedicated fiancé for refusing to give up on you. For going to the ends of the Earth to bring you home. For killing his enemies in the faint hope that you were still out there."

Ilya walks backward, his frame disappearing into the shadowed warehouse. Eventually, I can't see him, but I can hear his footsteps stop. A shifting of something heavy, and then the sound of something being dragged across the concrete. For the first time since I woke up in this room, I feel the pure, undiluted terror Ilya was hoping to inspire in me.

"And of course, her head will be evidence enough."

I know what I'll see before the light shines on her.

Ilya drags Emily by the scruff of her shirt, her limp body barely twitching as he tosses her on the floor in front of me. Horror slices through me, my blood feeling like it's made of ice shards as it pumps faster and faster through my veins. I'm so consumed with the sight of her, alive and groaning and obviously hurt, that I don't see where Ilya goes. But he comes back with a bucket in his hand, and a moment later he tosses the contents on her frame.

Emily gasps and chokes as what must be freezing water hits her skin. Her hands are bound behind her back, and her ankles together, but she rolls over to a sitting position as Ilya pulls a handgun from the small of his back and points it directly at her.

"Ilya, no, you don't understand," I say, my heart sinking with guilt over assuming she was in league with him. I didn't even consider that she could be his victim too. That she could be scared and alone, confused and tied up and at the whims of his icy rage.

All those weeks I spent worrying that she would be collateral damage, just for her to end up exactly where I feared she would be.

"Oh, I understand very clearly," he replies, with more

emotion than I've ever seen from him. I don't have time to unpack my confusion, to wonder why Emily angers him so.

"She's a researcher. We were working together. She has nothing to do with this," I beg, pleading for him to see the reason, even though I know he's not capable of it. Ilya is calculated, but once he sets his mind on a path, he is not easily deterred. Certainly not by the pleas of his fiancée.

"A researcher?" he repeats, a laugh erupting from him that leaves me frozen solid in disbelief. I've never heard him laugh. It sounds hollow and empty, like it's as unfamiliar to him as it is to me. "You know, for a moment I thought you had at least done something in your best interest. But you really are as stupid and useless as you look."

The words don't hurt the way they did last time, and I imagine the blows to come won't either. What is unbearable, though, is the way he looks at Emily. Like he knows her.

And if she's not working for him...

"Don't speak to her like that," Emily nearly growls, spitting at Ilya's feet. He cocks his head to the side, examining her like a rare specimen.

"She really doesn't know," he says in disbelief that matches mine. My head swivels between the two of them, trying to make sense of the scene before me.

"She's no one to me," I lie, assuming that Ilya's disdain for her stems from her touching what he considers his. "I didn't tell her anything."

"You know, I wish I could say I was impressed, but she threw herself at me like a common whore, so it doesn't take much," he says, ignoring me completely. Emily lunges, pulling against her restraints, pushing herself closer to the barrel Ilya extends toward her.

"Watch your mouth," she warns, staring down the barrel like she doesn't fear it at all. My Emily, who fears heights and depths, the unknown and the uncontrollable, is stalwart in the face of certain death.

"Or what, you'll cut my tongue out, too?" Ilya spits, releasing the safety of his gun with a definite click. Emily doesn't flinch. "I know your work well, Emily. Carlo may be the hand of that sanctimonious matriarch you serve, but you have a legacy all your own. The Snake of The Syndicate, they call you. Did you know that?"

I can't process what's happening in front of me. None of their words make sense. He can't know her.

"Cut off my head and three will grow back." She swears it like an oath, like a curse.

Who *is* she?

"We'll learn if that's true tonight," Ilya promises, tapping the barrel against her forehead.

"I don't..." I whisper, not really meaning to say the words aloud. Emily whips her head toward me, but Ilya keeps his eyes on her.

"Alice, I'm so sorry—"

The crack of Ilya's gun against her cheek silences her. I lunge forward, my chair nearly tipping over in my effort to get to her. A scream—her name—rips from my throat, but she says nothing at all. When she looks up again, she's licking away the blood dripping from her lip and coating her teeth. Her face doesn't reflect an ounce of pain or terror.

"Who are you?" I finally ask aloud.

"A pest," Ilya responds on her behalf, yanking Emily by her hair so she's further from me again. "And a deadly one."

"I wanted to explain," she says, staring at me like she needs me to know the truth of her words. "Last night—"

"She's a spy," Ilya cuts in, pushing the barrel of the gun, now spotted with her blood, against her temple again. Emily closes her eyes and breathes deeply through her nose. "A daughter of The Syndicate of Fate, a family of morally superior, meddlesome fools who imagine themselves superheroes. They believe themselves to be the only righteous villains in our world, and use their overblown sense of influence to dictate how our world operates."

"Influenced your brother right into an early grave," Emily mutters, earning another crack across the face. This time she smiles through it, but I can see the flicker of pain in her eyes. He might have broken her cheek, with how deep the gash is there.

Is Lev...did Emily kill Lev? My synapses are firing too fast to make any real sense of the words coming out of their mouths, but I know one thing for certain. I'm the least dangerous person in this room by a mile.

"I imagine Emily hid quite a bit about herself," Ilya taunts, somehow breaking my heart and making me feel unbearably naive at the same time. "She likely didn't mention that her fearless leader and aunt was nearly killed by your father a few years ago. Or that her little band of vindictive vigilantes have been trying to find ways into Konstantin's stronghold ever since."

Emily's gaze is locked on mine, and I know he's telling the truth, because they're filled with an apology she can't voice.

I feel another shard of whatever ice lives inside me now lodge into my lungs, making it even harder to breathe.

"She probably never mentioned that you two have met before."

Everything inside me feels cavernous. I'm empty, like a shell abandoned by its host on the sand. Losing my mother filled me with indescribable grief, which existed like a living, breathing thing for so long. But this? It is hollowing me into nothing at all.

"That's not possible," I say, the words broken from my lack of oxygen. I can't inhale. It hurts too much.

"You must remember Lucia Costa," Ilya chides, like I'm a forgetful child. Which is what I am to him. The name rings a distant bell, but I can't place it. "It was what, fifteen or so years ago, Emily? Konstantin invited her into your home to discuss a partnership. Short lived, those negotiations. But Lucia brought her niece with her."

I search my memory for Emily's face, but I come up empty. I would have been in my early teens, and I remember my mind was consumed with making my father proud. With earning his favor, and waking up to shiny new gifts as a token of his approval of my behavior.

I rarely looked around the rooms I was in. At the time, the only indulgence I provided myself was sneaking out to play—

"You brought it here?" I ask, certain she knows what I mean. Emily is silent for a few moments, but eventually she gives me the smallest nod.

She brought the viola to Nesika Beach. She sold it to the pawn shop so I could find it in the window. And she bought it back for me.

And I can't decide if it's the kindest or cruelest thing anyone has ever done to me.

"I imagine if you had given it a few more days, maybe a week or so, you would have found yourself in a very similar position to your current one, but with a different hand holding the gun," Ilya says, shrugging. I mean nothing to him, except the power I can bring him. My heartbreak is inconsequential to him.

"How could you?" I plead, not fully understanding if I mean the words coming out of my mouth. She looks equally anguished, her face crumpling under the weight of my words.

"Because that is who she is. That's who all of the Costas are," Ilya answers when Emily is silent. Finally, I break her gaze, looking up at my fiancé. He looks victorious.

I let the silence linger between us for a few more heartbeats, partly for Ilya's benefit, and partly because my mind is still trying to process the woman in front of me. Did she really come here to capture me on behalf of her family? If she did, what did she mean when she said she was doing her best not to be dangerous to me?

"How can I fix this, my husband?" I ask, bile rising in the back of my throat as I repeat the words he fed me. The gloating look on his face doesn't make it any better. Neither does Emily's soft *Alice*.

"See, I knew you'd see reason," Ilya patronizes, his praise so different from that Emily showered on me. He turns the barrel of his gun toward me for a moment before re-engaging the safety and slipping it back into his waistband. "First, you'll kill her. I don't like the idea of anyone alive having touched what I own."

I shake, because he expects me to. Because the thought of being the one to pull the trigger should be repugnant to Konstantin's sheltered daughter. And honestly, I don't have a bloodlust for anyone except my father and the man standing in front of me. Not even Emily, no matter how betrayed I feel right now.

"You'll endure a bit of pain, to prove how apologetic you are. And to show your father how ruthless the Costas can be. Why we should redouble our efforts to eliminate them." Nothing in his expression suggests he gets pleasure from causing pain, the way Lev did. "And then you will silently and *obediently* become my wife. This time, without complaints and mindless requests for accommodation."

"I don't want to get hurt again," I reply meekly, rounding my shoulders and letting my face fall. The memory of Ilya's causal, indifferent cruelty, the way he struck me and threw me against the wall without a shred of emotion, blankets my memory. I had come to him to ask for something—to go to an orchestral performance, if I remember correctly—and had argued when he denied me without explanation. "I'm sorry for last time. Please, I don't want to die. I won't argue, I promise."

Pathetic. Juvenile. Helpless.

Quiet. Subservient. Ornamental.

A needless object he can use to get what he wants, manipulate to ensure his legacy, and dispose of at his will. Just the type of wife Ilya wants. What he thinks he deserves.

I can't look at Emily. I could say it's because she lied to me, but I knew that was true before I got on that boat with her last night. Or because she was going to use me like Ilya is, a pawn in her own twisted, horrible plan. But I think it's because I can't witness her reaction to what comes next.

Ilya's fingers grasp my chin, pulling my gaze up to meet his. He scans each inch of my face, looking for deception or hesitation. But I don't have to fake the desperation seeping from every pore.

"If you lie to me, or try to escape, or tell anyone the truth, or anger me in any way, I will do worse than kill you," he swears, the grip on my face bruising, his nails cutting into my skin. "I will find every person you've spoken to in the last five years, every single one who helped you, knowingly or not. And I will skin them alive in front of you. So you can witness over and over again, the slow, painful death that awaits you for defying me. Do you understand?"

I think of Luanne and Jimmy and Alan. The rest of my mother's family, who I've never met but I know helped **Дядя** Mikhail coordinate my logistics in the States. The roommates in Portland, the woman who picked me up while hitchhiking in eastern Washington. Dozens of people who showed me an ounce of kindness.

I imagine them dead at my feet, because of me.

I promised myself that people would stop dying to keep me alive. And I'm going to keep that promise.

"I understand," I say, my voice shaking with determination that Ilya reads as terror.

"Good," he says, clearly pleased at my easy compliance. "Now show the snake that she is not special. That you'll hand your mouth over to anyone."

I wonder how long he was watching Emily and me. If he somehow saw us on the research boat or in her motel. Or if he assumed our intimacy based on the way he found us.

I look at her one last time, sitting back on her heels with chest caved in, tear tracks carving paths through the dirt on her face. For a fleeting moment, I let something other than fear fill my eyes. I try to tell her without words that she's the only person I've ever wanted. That tracing my mouth over her entire body is lightyears away from what I'm about to do. That even if I hate her now, I will always want her in a way I never wanted him.

I turn back to Ilya, all those feelings vanquished from my eyes, and let him seal his lips to mine.

Chapter 20
Emily

No.

This cannot be happening. What I'm seeing is impossible. I recognize that I've only known her for a few weeks, but deep down in my soul, I *know* that Alice would never go back to her father.

She told me so. On that cliff, under the bright, low-hanging moon. She all but said she'd rather die than reconcile. She doesn't value a life trapped, with no choice.

But here she is, kissing a man who will never love her, who will only use her for connection to Konstantin's power. Opening her mouth against his, letting his tongue sweep inside and erase every last trace of me. Letting him kiss her when I never was allowed to cement the memory of feeling her lips on mine.

When he pulls away, Ilya's gaze isn't hazy, his pupils aren't blown, his expression isn't adoring or even lust-ridden. He looks like he won. Like he's pinned and captured the prey he's been hunting.

My stomach clenches at that look. This is so much worse than the worst-case-scenario I imagined possible. Not only has

Ilya found Alice and me together, overwhelmed me physically so I couldn't protect her, and gotten me into a position that will most certainly end in my death, he also convinced her to turn back to her father.

I've lost everything. My life. My family. The only woman who has made me want anything for myself. And simultaneously, I've endangered the mission my family is dedicated to, putting Lucia and Clara and everyone who has loved me in far more danger than they ever have been, and I can't even warn them.

I'll be dead within the hour. And if I know Konstantin, he won't be the only one to see my head. He'll place it on my father and mother's doorstep, payback for Lev and all the other henchmen we've deposited in the forests surrounding his stronghold.

"Since this is your first kill, I'll make it easy for you," Ilya instructs patronizingly, reaching for his blade again. He cuts Alice's feet free first, keeping a hand on her body to hold her to the chair. He's strong—stronger than me—but I'm certain it's the threat of the violence his hand brings that keeps her in place.

When Ilya stands to start on her wrists he coughs once, his balance wavering for a moment. He swallows hard, steadying himself, and my eyes flicker to Alice. She's watching him carefully, that neutral, protective expression on her face again. Not nearly as afraid as she seemed moments ago.

"I'll put this gun in your hand, but don't think for a moment you can—" his monologue is cut off by another round of coughing. The hand holding the knife presses into his stomach, and he nearly doubles over.

I don't understand what's happening, but Alice seems to. Far in the distance, I hear a creak, almost completely covered by the sound of Ilya's hacking. Neither he nor Alice turn toward the sound, and I desperately pray it's not some wayward landlord or security guard coming to check out all the ruckus. I do not have the bandwidth for more innocent lives to protect.

"What did you do?" Ilya asks, brandishing his knife at Alice. I'd be worried for her safety, but Ilya looks like he's about to pass out, sweat dotting his forehead as he stumbles a few steps backwards. Alice maintains that carefully neutral expression, surveying his every twitch like I would a research subject in my lab back in Boston. What *did* she do?

"Me?" she asks, adopting the patronizing, sardonic tone Ilya was using on her. "How could I do anything, Ilya? I'm nothing but a tool at your disposal."

He sways on his feet again, reaching for the small of his back but missing his gun. I fear he's going to start shooting wildly, or lunging at us with that very sharp blade. He may be inexplicably disoriented, but I'm still bound, no matter how hard I try to slip my wrists from the snare.

A struggle Alice apparently does not share, because she's standing in front of him now, hands completely free from the rope that lays on the ground behind her chair. Ilya swipes wildly toward her, but she dodges easily. He stumbles over the empty bucket he used to rouse me, the clanging of metal on concrete so unnaturally loud as it echoes through this empty warehouse. I hear steps to my nine o'clock, and I pray to all the saints my father ever told me of that a friendly—or at least, familiar—face is here.

Alice spits on Ilya's face, and he turns to vomit on the floor next to him.

"You spoiled...deranged little...bitch," Ilya curses through heaves and gags, the stench of bile and rotten food permeating the room. I hold back a gag, but Alice seems completely unaffected.

"You really shouldn't have used a knot my father taught

you," she chides, stepping on his hand until he lets go of the blade clutched in it with a cry. She kicks it away, though far from where I'm still bound, which is both annoying and informative. She doesn't want me free.

Reasonable.

"I hope this death is slow and painful," she whispers at him, using her bare foot to push his hip up. He tries to grab at her leg, but she easily shakes him off, flipping him over on his stomach with a hard kick. "I hope your organs fail inside your body slowly, so you can taste the blood that will drown you. I hope you beg for death, like you made so many others do without mercy. And I hope you feel every ounce of the fear and pain I did when you told me I'd die just like my mother—used until worthless."

Ilya's shallow, gasping breaths, broken only by gagging and coughing, fill the warehouse and echo off the walls as Alice leans down and pulls the handgun from his waistband. I wonder what the fuck our shadowed visitor is waiting for as Alice rolls her shoulders, cracks her neck, and turns the gun on me.

"Explain."

Despite my confusion, fear, nausea, pain, and a thousand other feelings rolling around in my chest, I can't help but notice how good Alice looks with a gun in her hand.

"I don't think I'm the only one who has some explaining to do," I accuse, raising my eyebrows at Ilya's twitching, writhing frame. Alice looks unaffected.

"*I think* I'm the only one with a gun," she replies cooly, disengaging the safety to make her point. Kinda hot.

"That's where you're wrong."

Oh thank god, it's Bea.

Alice swivels in place, aiming her weapon right where Bea is emerging from the shadows. I look over my shoulder and throw her a grin that's meant to convey *oops, sorry, fucked up pretty bad here, please don't kill her.*

"Who the hell are *you?*" Alice demands, her aim unwavering and not an ounce of fear in her eyes as she faces the barrel of Bea's gun. I'm starting to think the quivering, helpless act was all for Ilya's benefit.

"My cousin," I say, before Bea shoots back some half-answer that will only piss Alice off more. I think we're past subterfuge at this point.

"I suppose I don't have to ask if what he said was true, then," she bites, glaring at me like she'd kill me with the look if she could.

"He left some key details out, which I'd like to explain, if possible," I plead, watching Bea out of the corner of my eye. I don't exactly trust her not to kill Alice on the spot, utility to our mission be damned.

"She gets her explanation when we get ours," Bea says with finality, raising Alice's hackles. Which, of course, was Bea's goal. Ever the instigator.

"I think I'm owed a bit more than that, seeing as I've apparently been used as a disposable pawn between your family and my father for the last few weeks," she argues, keeping her aim true, right at Bea's forehead. I wonder how much weapons training her father provided her. Apparently he taught her to escape having her wrists bound, which redirects my mind to quite inappropriate and unlikely possibilities.

"You're actually quite a useful pawn, if that makes you feel better." I'm going to kill Bea.

"Okay, okay, let's calm the verbal sparring," I ask as Alice takes a step closer to my cousin. I don't doubt that Bea is quicker to the trigger than Alice is, but rage will do a lot for a woman, including making her impulsive. And I really don't need either of them to shed blood today. "Bea, let me explain.

Ilya told her about The Syndicate, so there's no point in keeping secrets now."

Bea's glance toward me tells me she thinks there are *plenty* of reasons for secrets, but I ignore her, turning back to Alice and hoping neither of them choose to shoot me instead.

"Ilya was right," I start, another round of vomiting from the man himself punctuating my confession. "The Costas, my family, are the central core of an enterprise known as The Syndicate of Fate. We work within and through other criminal enterprises to carry out our mission. It's a complicated family history, but we currently are trying to cut off some of the larger international human trafficking operations. We don't work within existing legal channels, but I feel *sanctimonious* was a little harsh."

Neither Alice nor Bea laughs at my joke, which hangs in the air like the heavy stench of puke. Brilliant.

"I assume my father was on your hit list," she guesses, not seeming particularly perturbed by the concept.

"Only recently," Bea cuts in, still aiming her gun at Alice. "Years ago, we tried to form a partnership. He's a savvy and charismatic man, and we knew he would climb the ranks and find a following in the world of weapons trade and transfer. We'd hoped he could be persuaded to use his expanding network to help monitor human trafficking operations through the ports he had influence over, and in exchange, we would ensure he faced little competition regionally from other gun runners."

"What superheroes," Alice says sarcastically, her cutting gaze flicking to me before returning to Bea and the threat she wields.

"I told you, we're not altruistic. We have a goal, and we use whatever avenues are open to us to achieve it," I argue, earning an eye roll, which is rich coming from the girl who used to wear diamonds bought with blood-soaked rubles.

"Konstantin was uninterested in such a partnership," Bea continues, like there was no interruption at all. "He wanted more out of The Syndicate than we were willing to offer, and saw better opportunities for increasing his power and influence by joining the forces we were trying to fight. Negotiations fell apart pretty quickly."

"So he tried to kill your leader." It's not a question. Alice says it like it's a predictable outcome of interacting with her father.

"Not until about two years ago," I say, earning a glare from Bea. But I no longer care. I refuse to lie to Alice about anything anymore. "You had already been assumed dead for almost three years, and your father had expanded his operations significantly in that time. Our Matriarch focused more pointedly on curtailing his influence, turning his operatives to our side or killing the ones who refused."

We're all quiet for a moment as Alice processes what she's learning, her brow furrowed over the horizon of the metal in her hand.

"How did you know I was alive?" she asks, more curious than accusatory.

"We're very good at our jobs," Bea says, cryptic as fuck for no reason.

"We learned that Konstantin had Mikhail killed, and followed Ilya's movements for a few weeks before realizing what he was looking for," I explain more thoroughly. "Bea had heard the rumors that you had been smuggled out, and we put the pieces together until we found you."

"And what exactly were you going to do with me, after you stalked me and fucked me and kidnapped me?" Alice demands, her voice much less neutral than it was a moment ago. Bea's lips twitch into the shadow of a smile before she covers it.

"Emily will answer that question when you explain *that*," Bea negotiates, waving her gun at Ilya's frame. His back is still rising and falling, and every once in a while a muffled groan slips from his lips, so he's still alive.

"Rattlesnake venom," Alice responds with a shrug, opening her mouth wide in our direction. "A capsule hidden in a loose cap."

"And why aren't you half dead on the ground?" I ask, stupified by the fact that Alice just happened to have a capsule of fucking *snake venom* in her mouth when—

"Mithridatism," Bea answers on her behalf, clearly and begrudgingly impressed. "Clever, if unpredictable."

"Wait a minute, is that why you wouldn't let me kiss you? You had that fucking thing in your mouth the whole time?" I whip my head back and forth between Alice and my cousin, slightly annoyed that they seem to be sizing each other up while I'm tied to the ground next to the nearly-dead guy. "You planned this. You knew he was coming and you prepared!"

"Oh, I think you'll find that Alice did more than predict Ilya's arrival. She ensured it."

Now Bea seems *unabashedly* impressed. And I'm thoroughly irritated.

"It wasn't enough to kill him quickly," Alice explains, glancing over her shoulder at Ilya's limp, curled up frame. "But I'd prefer he die slowly, if possible."

"I'd prefer to be cut free from this fucking rope, if possible," I grumble, especiallly perturbed when Bea and Alice both reply *no* at the same time.

"So what comes next?"

I'm surprised the question comes from Bea, not Alice. It's like my cousin is testing her, seeing if she is able to move her own pieces on this chessboard, rather than be a pawn in the game.

Alice stares at me like she wishes she could ask a hundred questions at once. She doesn't lie to me anymore either, and the pain and betrayal I see in her eyes makes me feel worse than I would if I were in Ilya's shoes right now.

"I suppose it's time to figure out how valuable I am to you."

Chapter 21
Alice

An hour later, Beatrice—whose name I learned only after we agreed to holster our weapons—and I had made quite a bit of progress. We moved Ilya and propped him up against the wall of the warehouse so he didn't choke on his own puke, found the switch to turn on more lights, and even filled the bucket a few times over so we could wash his putrid vomit down a nearby drain.

Emily's hands and feet are still bound, much to her chagrin. Bea was kind enough to help her into the metal folding chair. I think she's getting a kick out of seeing Emily helpless.

As we cleaned, Emily explained the plan she and her cousins had concocted for me. How she manipulated her PhD program funding so she could research where she knew I was hiding. Her directive from Clara—her eldest cousin and the next leader of their weird vigilante criminal-yet-crime-fighting enterprise—was to get information about my father's operations out of me and determine if I could be used as bait to lure him out of Vladivostok. She emphasized how she advocated for me to be brought under the protection of The Syndicate, to be told the whole truth and given a choice.

"Exactly *how much* choice would I have had if you brought me in?" I asked, pointing the question more toward Bea than Emily. "If she had told me the truth about The Syndicate, and I didn't want to cooperate, what would have happened?"

She'd assessed me for a few heartbeats before shrugging.

"We may have killed you, though I'm starting to think Emily would have done almost anything to prevent that. Likely, we would have used you against your will to lure out your father."

Well, at least I can be fairly certain Bea isn't lying to me.

"It wouldn't have worked," I tell them when there's no more work to keep our hands and minds busy. Emily sits up straighter in her chair, and Bea rolls her eyes. "Using me as bait. My father doesn't know I'm alive, but even if he did, he wouldn't risk his own life to save mine. Doesn't matter if he thought I was a traitor or a victim."

"What if he thought you were a liability?" Bea asks. The question actually gives me pause. I'd never really thought of that possibility before.

"I don't know a lot about my father's operations. Obviously I was aware of his work, and I have had some basic self defense and informational training so I could be a good wife to Ilya, and mother to the heirs we'd produce, but nothing that would make him vulnerable. You likely know him better than I do."

I shrug, but the strange pit in my stomach is hard to ignore. I'm not even useful to the people who wanted to kidnap me. After all this, the only place I've ever had purpose is under the thumb of the men of my father's empire. It's a sickening realization.

"You'd be surprised," Bea replies, her voice a touch more gentle than it's been since I've met her. She's very cold and matter-of-fact, but in a way that feels refreshing and cutting, rather than cruel like Ilya. "Often, a person's most vulnerable qualities are shared without them even realizing."

Speaking of vulnerability...

"Bea, would you mind giving us a few minutes?" Emily asks, her expression half grimace, half pleading grin and she stares up at her cousin.

"I would mind, actually," Bea replies, and I have to choke back a laugh. "You haven't earned much latitude in this situation, Emily."

The grimace wins out at those words. Emily's eyes flicker toward me, conflicted and pained.

"Fair. But I'll request you don't tell Clara what you're about to hear."

"We'll see about that," Bea mutters, turning toward Ilya to check his vitals and eavesdrop.

Emily, still with her hands bound behind her back and ankles to one another, looks nothing short of pathetic as she turns her whole body toward me. Every inch of her, from her posture to the pleading look in her eyes, feels like a confession. I haven't had to face the riot of emotions filling my lungs, replacing oxygen molecule by molecule. But now, I can't breathe without tasting bitter betrayal and sweet black licorice.

"I know you have no reason to trust me, but I had a plan," she says earnestly, rushing the words out like she's afraid I'll run from her before I hear her side of the story. "I wanted to tell you everything last night. But then..." She glances over her shoulder at Bea, who isn't at all pretending not to listen, but is instead staring directly at Emily. "Well, you asked for what you wanted. And I wanted to give you complete control."

"Don't make your lies my fault," I demand, my voice much stronger than I feel. "You lied to me from the moment we met. The only time you were completely honest with me was when there was a gun to your head. You're right, there's no reason for me to trust you."

And yet, I hate that I want to. In the very depths of me, all I want is to trust her. To lay my head on her chest and listen to her heartbeat. To put my tired hand in hers and know she'll lead me toward safety. To trust that she'll give me control when I need it, and take it when I can't handle the weight on my shoulders any longer.

"Please tell me you don't think that." She sounds as heartbroken as I am. "I swear, I only lied about the things I absolutely had to. Every time I had the opportunity to tell you the truth, to be vulnerable with you, I took it."

"And that's supposed to be enough?" I ask, my voice shaking against my will. I wish I could say it was rage making the words unstable, but it's something far more pitiful. "I'm supposed to be forgive you for lying through your teeth because you told me you were afraid of the fucking ocean?"

She opens and closes her mouth a few times, and I can see every apology in her eyes. Read the *forgive me* and *please trust me* like she's written them in her blood on the concrete beneath us.

But she never voices them.

Instead, her body shifts. She straightens her shoulders, all the supplication gone. In its place is the predatory confidence I saw last night.

It makes my skin flash, and my eyes flicker to Bea, who's leaning against the wall and watching us like a public performance.

"A little hypocritical, don't you think?" Emily asks, leaning forward in her chair to get as close to me as she can without standing. My instinct is to take a step backward, but I hold my ground.

"Excuse me?" I respond, proud that the indignation in my voice hasn't been replaced with something more revealing.

"You're not fragile," she says, and I don't know how she makes those words sound seductive, like a siren's call. "So I'm not going to treat you like you are."

"I don't—" I start, but she immediately cuts me off.

"You lied to me as much as I lied to you," she accuses, and I clench my jaw, my tongue sliding to the unfamiliar gap in the back of my mouth nervously. She notices. Because of course she does. "You had no idea who I was. As far as you were aware, I was a researcher in the wrong place at the wrong time. And you lied about your entire life, making me trust you when you were drawing danger closer and closer every day."

"You think we're even then?" I bite back, taking a step closer to her so she has to crane her neck to meet my gaze. It doesn't make her any less intimidating. "I did what I had to do to protect myself. You did what you had to do to *use* me."

And I'm not wrong. Her sins are greater than mine.

But we both put each other in danger. We both prioritized our missions, the things we needed to protect ourselves and get revenge on the same man, over each other. When we first met, I would have said that Emily and I couldn't be more different. Her strength to my weakness, her anxiety to my fearlessness, her need for control to my desire for freedom. But it's clear now that at the core of us, we are cut from the same cloth.

"Bea, tell Alisa what would have happened if I didn't bring her to Clara," Emily requests. I jolt at the reminder that I'm still not safe. That a half-dead Ilya in the corner is only half my battle, and the two Costa cousins in front of me may still use me to lure my father into the open. I shift and feel slightly comforted by the warm metal of a barrel tucked into the band of my sweatpants. It's likely naive to believe I could outdraw

Bea, but at least I'd go down swinging, as the Americans like to say.

"You would have been excommunicated from The Syndicate of Fate. A public award would have been placed on your head, and each member of your family would be tasked with hunting you down and bringing you home for punishment."

Bea doesn't seem affected by this horrid explanation, but I suppose she hasn't been affected by much in the short time I've known her. I, however, feel my pulse in my fingertips, and I cross my arms over my chest, digging my nails into skin to avoid acknowledging her words.

"You brought Bea here. You weren't running from them, you were calling in reinforcements," I spit out. Emily's confident, almost lazy grin should be infuriating. I cannot stand that I find it attractive. Something is wrong with me.

"Not to defend my irrational, hardheaded cousin, but she in fact did *not* call me in," Bea corrects, the first hint of something like humor coloring her tone. "Clara sent me because Emily couldn't be trusted to complete her mission independently."

I don't want to believe them.

I *really* want to believe them.

"Ask her why I couldn't be trusted," Emily says, her confidence cracking slightly, letting desperation bleed through. I can't look at her, so I keep my eyes on Bea.

"No," I say, my voice too quiet to be convincing.

"Tell her, Bea," Emily directs. Bea pushes her long, dark hair over her shoulder, raising her eyebrows at the back of Emily's head.

"She doesn't want to know."

"Yes, she does," Emily says, and I can feel her gaze on my cheek, my neck, my lips. "She knows what to say if she really didn't want to hear it."

I could say it. It would be a test of Emily's willingness to listen, to maintain boundaries, to stop when I really need her to.

But I don't want that word to be associated with these kinds of tests anymore. In the darkest parts of me, where the woman I will be when my father is dead resides, I only want to use that word how it was meant to be used. To take a breath with the person who makes it easier to breathe.

Bea waits a few heartbeats.

"She put your life before the mission," she says. Her face is carefully neutral now. Not the easy indifference I've seen her wear so far. I know what it looks like when someone is hiding beneath their own skin, and that's what Bea is doing. "She implied that sacrificing you to your father was inherently contradictory to The Syndicate's values, regardless of his actions against us. It was clear she'd compromise our ability to enact our retribution if it meant risking you."

I swallow hard. My heart feels like it's beating in my throat, choking me, making it impossible to respond, even if I knew what to say.

It's wrong to let my own weakness and insecurity drive my feelings about Emily. She lied to me, manipulated me, used me. Just because she was allegedly willing to give up her entire life, everyone and everything she valued, to keep me safe, doesn't justify her dishonesty and exploitation.

But there's a small, jagged, broken part of me that desperately wants someone who will sacrifice everything for me. The little girl who only wanted to be something more than a pawn, finally becoming someone's queen, their most valuable and treasured piece.

Perhaps it's toxic. An extension of the objectification that my father and Ilya and everyone else that raised and groomed me required. But the queen can move any way she wants on the chessboard. And I have to hope that's a step in the right direction.

"I don't forgive you," I say, the exhaustion and pain I've been withholding finally staking its claim on my body. My shoulders sag as I look at Emily, still bound and in her chair.

"You shouldn't," she says, and I believe she means it. "But I'd like the opportunity to earn it. And to forgive you too, for nearly getting me killed by your ex."

Bea moves quicker than I can blink and smacks Emily on the back of the head.

And for the first time in what feels like a lifetime, I laugh.

Chapter 22
Emily

"**I** should fucking kill *both* of you!"

Clara's voice is muffled by the closed door at the end of the hallway, but she's screaming loud enough for me to hear pretty clearly. I drag my hands down my face and lean back against Bea's couch, rubbing my eyes with the heels of my palms.

"Could be worse. We could both be dead already."

Alice's voice next to me is the only thing bringing me comfort. The feeling of her thigh inches from mine. And her smell—sea salt and blackberries, like I knew it would be, even far from that boat.

The whispers of my family hiding in Bea's dining area are certainly not calming me. Charlie, Gwen, and Deniz sit very far away, glancing over at Alisa and I surreptitiously. Well, it *would* be surreptitiously, if they weren't less than fifty fucking feet from us.

"Death might be preferable."

My statement is validated by the shattering of glass behind the closed door at the end of the hall.

It's only been four days since Ilya took us from that boat,

but it feels like a lifetime. Bea and I got as much out of Ilya as we could, considering his organs were deteriorating rapidly. But even in that state, he had quite a bit more fortitude than his younger brother did. Whether because the poison addled his mind, or because he was unwilling to be a traitor to Konstantin, even in death, he gave us very little.

Which, of course, was not going to make things any better with Clara.

Bea had insisted that we proceed as directed—bring Alice to her townhouse in Tokyo, explain what happened, try to convince her not to excommunicate us and throw us to literal wolves.

It seems like Bea is on my side, but that may be more Alice's doing than mine. Of all my cousins, Bea and I have always been the most distant. She's so much more serious than I ever was, calm in the face of everything that startled me, emotionally detached when I was shaken. I resented her for how easily she seemed to fit into this life.

I think she resented me for how gentle my parents were with me.

But I think Bea sees a bit of herself in Alice. Someone who lost one parent that was supposed to coddle and care for them, and was left to endure the pain of the other who prioritized work over anything else.

All that to say, she could be throwing me under the bus right now, locked in that office with Clara. It was quite the scene when the rest of our family arrived at the townhouse I'd never set foot in. Alice and I stood in the corner, my body instinctively covering hers as Charlie, Gwen, Deniz, and Clara were led in by Bea. I swear I saw Clara's hand twitch for her waistband, but she was blessedly unarmed. She might have lunged at me, tried to kill me with her bare hands, if it wasn't for Deniz's arm around her shoulder and Bea tugging on her elbow toward the office.

There's been quite a lot of yelling over the past two hours.

Currently, there's some particularly loud murmuring from the dining table. I don't remove my palms from my eyes until I hear footsteps headed our way.

Deniz stands in front of us, staring down at Alice. His eyes are narrowed, but more from curiosity than suspicion, if I could guess. He doesn't give me a second glance, and neither does Alice. Deniz can be an intimidating guy, but my brave girl doesn't cower, as per the usual.

"Your fiancé killed my brother," Deniz says bluntly, his lips pressing into a thin line as he takes a deep breath. "Your father ordered the assassination that ended his life."

I watch Alice carefully, but she doesn't flinch. It's not the unaffected, glazed facade she dons to hide herself. It's an honest, raw understanding of the man who raised her, and the one she was promised to.

"My father has enough blood on his hands to color the ocean red," she says. Her fingers twitch on the couch beside me, but she doesn't reach for my hand. "I'm sorry he took your brother from you. He took my mother from me, too. I hope we both get to avenge them one day."

Deniz's expression doesn't change. He simply watches Alice for a few moments more. They have some silent conversation, battle of wills or test of character. After a few tense beats, Deniz nods and turns back to the table with Charlie and Gwen.

Charlie looks at me like he has no fucking clue what's going on, his eyebrows permanently furrowed and raised toward his hairline. Gwen is looking at me like I'm an idiot.

I think we should stop having family reunions. They're never much fun.

Suddenly, the door at the end of the hall slides open. Clara steps out first, steam almost visibly rising from her ears as she stalks into the living room. The only one brave enough to get close to her is Deniz, drawn like an object in her gravitational pull. He floats to her side as she finds her place in the center of the room, even as the rest of my family slinks further against the wall.

I don't blame them. I'd like to be out of her trajectory right now, too.

"You two are going to answer my questions with a simple yes or no," she demands, brokering no room for argument. Alice is immediately on edge, maybe even a little frightened. She shifts toward me, keeping her wary eyes on Clara's hands. Good to know my cousin is objectively more terrifying than both an international arms dealer and human trafficker.

"What if—"

"I swear on Nonno's grave, Emily, if you say another word other than *yes* or *no* I will put a bullet between your eyes."

I want to say that I wasn't trying to be difficult, that I was only going to explain what happened in my own words, but I'm smart enough to seal my lips.

"Finally putting all those fucking degrees to work," she mutters, rollling her neck. Deniz is standing precariously close to her, like he anticipates having to hold her back. Fantastic.

"Before you were kidnapped by Andreeva—which is pathetic, by the way. You let him catch you unaware? Your mother would kill you," she reproves, frustration evident in every syllable. "Did you intend to tell Alisa Zakharov about The Syndicate of Fate and your mission, and in doing so, jeopardize our operation?"

I don't look at Bea. She may understand why I did what I did, but she wouldn't lie to her Matriarch. She's second only to Clara in her steadfast and undying dedication to The Syndicate.

Instead, I look directly in her eyes. I don't show fear, because I don't feel it. If I have to die for the truth, so be it.

"Yes."

Clara's nostrils flare, and I can hear the breath hiss out of her in the silence of the room. She takes a few beats and turns to Alice.

"And did you intentionally lure Ilya Andreeva out of Russia in order to poison and kill him?"

"Yes," Alice replies quickly, not a single drop of hesitation or guilt in her voice.

"Did you realize how ill-formed and ill-fated your plan was?"

Alice bites the inside of her cheek, probably reminding herself that she didn't survive murdering her ex only to die because she couldn't keep her mouth shut.

"Yes," she admits rather ruefully, an annoyed lilt to the words.

Clara takes a few more deep breaths, controlled and careful, like she's diffusing a bomb. Her own temper, I suppose.

"I would like to make it clear that you are both currently breathing because Bea has convinced me of your utility to our plan, and for no other reason. After Konstantin is dead, you will face the council's judgement, as our edicts require, Emily. You could still lose your position in The Syndicate. Or worse."

I nod my head slowly, a little afraid to say *I understand* out loud. Clara's eyes flash, but she turns back to Alice.

"You have proven, at least to Beatrice, that you harbor no loyalty to your father or his people. I hope you know that we trust no one but each other, and that includes you. Everyone in this room will be watching your every move, and if you give the slightest inkling that you are an enemy, you will be killed without question. Do you understand?"

Alice has lived this life before—constantly being watched,

needing to prove her loyalty to those who are supposed to protect her. A little flicker of disappointment flashes in her eyes, but she nods all the same.

"Yes."

The tension in Clara's shoulders loosens, and the room releases a collective sigh of relief when we realize she's not about to kill me or Alice. Deniz takes the opportunity to place his hand at the small of her back, prompting her to lean into him. It's small, but I've never seen Clara rely on *anyone* for *anything*. It's strange, like an uncanny valley version of the vicious, hyper-independent badass I've always known.

"You know, you've really fucked this all up Emily," she scolds, morphing from Matriarch to cousin Clara in a matter of seconds. She turns to find a chair, and the rest of the Costas and their partners cautiously join her at the table. Charlie gives me a look that clearly says *get over here now, you idiot*, so I grab Alice by the elbow and bring her with me. I stick her between Gwen and I, since that seems like the safest open seat.

"I do know that," I admit, injecting an unfamiliar but honest humility into my tone. "If it helps, I plan on abdicating my position within The Syndicate the moment Konstantin is dead."

"What?"

It's not Clara, or either of my other cousins, who voices the question. It's Alice, whose bewildered face is turned up at me.

"You ran from this life. I won't survive if you run from me. Leaving is the only choice."

It was a very simple decision I made on the flight to Tokyo. We both need time to heal from the lies and manipulation we subjected each other to. And to be frank, I knew I had a lot of work to do in order to get Alice to forgive me—work I couldn't do if I was chasing her around the world as she fled a life filled with blood and victims and countless other horrible things. It might be easy to track her down, knowing what I do about her now, but it wouldn't allow us to fix things. To get to know each other. To forgive and maybe begin anew.

"You know, you really haven't learned anything, have you?" Alice says, the words and the sadness in her eyes cutting directly into my chest, leaving me exposed and raw.

"Alice, I was trying—"

"No, you're *choosing*," she says, cutting me off with my mouth still hanging open. "For me. You know the thing I want most in the world, and you're denying me the chance to have it because you're stubbornly trying to control the outcome of us."

I can't focus on how everyone else at the table reacts. All I can see is the hurt on Alice's face, and the guilt that immediately swallows me whole.

She's not wrong. I want so badly to mold every moment from here on out so I can guarantee she'll be standing by my side at the end of all this. Because I need her. The very essence of my body and soul is tied to Alice, and I've never feared anything more than the idea of losing her. To death, to hatred, to anything.

I hear her words from a few days ago, floating to the forefront of my mind like they were brought in with the tide. *This isn't about facing your fears. It's about learning that fear isn't necessary.*

I have to believe she meant it. That there's still a thread of something good and beautiful stitching us together.

"Okay, how about we discuss it once we kill your father?"

For a second, I think she'll break with laughter. But she adopts her normal deadpan disdain for my overconfidence, huffing a breath through her nose.

"I'll think about it," she replies, and my lungs fill with breathable air again.

That's not a no. It's certainly not a *jellyfish.*

"You two are worse than us," Gwen mutters, elbowing Charlie in the bicep. He winks at her before surveying the table.

"I think it's a family trait, the toxic relationships," he offers, eyeing Deniz who seems completely unperturbed. Actually, he seems to take it as a badge of honor.

"Are you calling your Matriarch's impending marriage *toxic*, Carlo?" Clara asks, using a hint of her *matriarch* voice as she chides her brother. He gives her an apologetic look, but doesn't retract his statement.

"I think we deserve to hear the rest of the story," Gwen says, scooting closer to Alice. She takes her in like a research subject, like an animal in a cage she's supposed to observe for science. "I have a million questions."

"I'm sure you do," I mutter, earning a kick from Charlie. Alice's cheeks flush a bit, unused to having this many people speak to her at the same time.

"I'm not sure where to start," she admits, tucking her hair behind her ears.

"Well, I've got a question," Bea starts, pushing off the wall and placing her palms on the table so she can lean toward Alice. The smallest smile pulls at the corner of her lips. "How in the world did you get rattlesnake venom with no access to the internet?"

And the grin that stretches across Alice's face is the most beautiful I've ever seen.

Chapter 23
Alice

Three Weeks Later

"Once more."

Nobuko's voice is soft yet stern, her eyes closed as she waits for me to start again. I place the familiar warm wood of my viola—the same one Emily bought for me twice—under my chin and set the bow against the strings.

I have no idea how Emily got one of the most acclaimed violists alive today to give me lessons, but it seems like her family has endless connections, and I'm not complaining. I play through the piece again, the rhythm so familiar now that I move on muscle memory alone.

My technique is rusty, but the feeling is still there, finally breathing after years of being buried inside me. Music was once my escape, my form of rebellion. But now it feels like I have much less to escape from. Music can be a part of almost any moment I want, rather than only those I keep to myself.

The last few weeks have been...strange. The Costas don't

know what to do with me, but they clearly agree on one thing—we must keep the fact that I'm alive a secret, from my father and the world. To that end, I've been staying in a small but comfortable apartment in Mitaka. It took a few days and about a dozen conversations that felt more like interrogations, but eventually Clara allowed Emily to set me up a private space, under the close and invisible watch of about a dozen Syndicate employees, of course.

For my protection. And to ensure I don't run.

I suppose I can't blame them for the extra precaution. I did fake my death to escape a multinational criminal enterprise once before.

The final notes of the piece resonate through my fingers, and I realize I've closed my eyes—feeling, more than reading, the music on the stand before me. Nobuko seems pleased, smile restrained but eyes shimmering with understanding.

"You're improving," she says simply, a compliment from a giant in this world. "Practice more, especially at the recapitulation."

I carefully lay my instrument in its case, which is much newer and shinier, at the end of our lesson, feeling like there's helium filling my lungs. Every time I play, or even see my viola in its case, it's like a hallucination. Part of me can't believe that my life has changed so much so quickly, that this beautiful piece of art is mine.

My steps are quick and heavy down the narrow stairwell, and I stumble onto the busy sidewalk, pressing my body against the side of the building to avoid being trampled. It's rush hour, and after years of relative isolation in Vladivostok, and the otherworldly quiet of Nesika Beach, the overwhelming noise of downtown Tokyo sets me on edge.

I lift onto my toes, craning my neck to find a familiar car

idling on the side of the road. She's never late. Not to pick me up at my apartment, not to drop me off for my lessons, and not to retrieve me when I'm ready to leave.

Emily is smiling, tall and stunning as she holds the passenger door open. My viola case presses against my chest as I snake through the crowd and slip into the seat—the noise blessedly muffled when the door closes.

"Where to?" she asks from back behind the wheel. I still haven't learned to drive, and I think it'll be a long time before that's a priority. There are trains from Mitaka, but Emily has insisted that she's happy to take me wherever I want to go. And I've let her.

"Remember the place with the sweet chili tofu?" I ask, my stomach growling as if on cue. The corner of Emily's mouth lifts as she puts the car in gear.

"You got it."

She navigates through the heavy traffic as I people-watch through the window. As much as the noise of a big city is overwhelming, I've loved observing the world around me in a new way. Instead of looking for my father or Ilya in a crowd, I let myself soak in everything I've missed before. The outfits people wear, the advertisements on the train, the neon lights of signs and displays. It's likely because I know there's someone—or quite a few someones, an entire network of someones— protecting me. But for the first time in half a decade, I don't feel like I'm on alert. I just *live*.

"Good lesson today?" Emily asks, the same question she's posed after my last two. I tap my fingernails against my viola case, tucked between my feet.

"Harder today, but that's a good thing," I reply, recalling the uncomfortable but rewarding feeling of being pushed, of Nobuko demanding more of me, and meeting that challenge. The helium fills my chest again.

"I'm glad you're enjoying it," she whispers, and I know she means it. She was worried that playing again would be too difficult for me, or that I'd have a reaction similar to when I first saw the viola in the window of the pawn shop. I was, too. But after the initial shock waned, all I could feel was an unending desire to play more, to be better, to remember. I practice far more diligently than I ever did as a girl.

The drive is quiet, like it often is, and it's almost an hour before we get back to the neighborhood my temporary home is in. Emily parks in a small lot behind the restaurant I now recognize, and is out of the car and opening my door for me before I can even get my seatbelt off.

She doesn't hold my hand, because I haven't asked her to. She doesn't touch me unless I initiate it, even platonically. She's kept her promise to let me choose, whenever choice is possible.

"Same thing as last time?" Emily asks when we're seated in a low-lit booth at the back of the restaurant. The waiter responded to most of our questions in English, regardless of the language we asked them in, smiling kindly and placing transcribed menus in front of us. Neither of us are fluent in Japanese, and mine is certainly worse than Emily's, but Bea has given us some basic lessons the few times I've seen her. Like when she magically turned up at the apartment with everything I left behind in Oregon, plus some new clothes and toiletries. Or the evening when she showed up to ask me about whales.

"I think so, but I liked the eggplant you got too," I ruminate, flipping the menu over and scanning my options. Emily will likely order both for me, and then tell me it's better left over anyway, and demand I take the to-go boxes home.

It's odd, knowing some parts of a person so well, while completely in the dark about others.

When the waiter returns to take our order, Emily wordlessly confirms she can order for me before requesting a small feast of options.

She's trying. Every day, I can see it. Little moments and big ones where she defers to me, asks for my opinion, prioritizes my feelings.

I forgave her a while ago. Probably the moment I realized she was wholeheartedly planning on abdicating The Syndicate for me. But the opportunity to build this quiet little world of trust and gentleness between us, when we're surrounded by endless chaos and violence, has been too good to give up.

The restaurant is fairly empty, and a few of the patrons seem familiar. Probably the Syndicate spies contracted to keep tabs on me. Still, I know better than most that eyes and ears live in the shadows.

Which is why I lean in close, my chest pressed against the thick wood of the table.

"I would like to know more."

Emily's eyes scan my face, centimeter by centimeter. She does this a lot, and I'm not always sure what she's looking for. Sometimes I think she may be looking at me for the hell of it.

"How much more?" she asks, taking a careful sip of her water. I place my hands beneath my knees so I won't drum my fingers nervously.

"More than you can tell me, probably."

Three weeks doesn't seem long, but in a world like Emily's, I know time moves quickly. I've cooperated with Clara and the rest of her family's inquisition so far, but I know that's only the beginning.

During one of her late-night visits, Bea explained my options. I knew too much about The Syndicate to ever fully be free of them. But I could decide I didn't want to walk their path of vengeance toward my father. They would set me up somewhere with a normal job in a normal city, and while I'd forever be under their surveillance, I would barely notice their existence. I'd be protected, but separated. Safe, but alone.

Or, I could join them. When I asked Bea what that entailed, she had been purposefully and infuriatingly vague. *I think that's up to you*, she had mused, eating the last of my crackers and leaving crumbs on my counter. *You, and perhaps Emily.*

"There are..." she trails off, her eyes darting through the shadows of the restaurant. "There are degrees to this, in a way. Depending on how involved you want to be. How much you trust us."

She says *us*, but I know she means *me*. Her expression is filled with such trepidation. Hope and caution in equal measure swim in her eyes as she places her hands flat on the table, palms down. Like she's searching for stability.

Emily lied to me, many times. But she did it for the people she loves. And when I lay in my bed at night and wonder if her lies are too much to overcome, I think about the moment Ilya dragged her limp, battered body in front of me. How I lied through my teeth to save her, telling him she was no one, a researcher who meant nothing to me, in the slimmest hope that he would spare her.

And I imagine far worse things I would say and do for her. For the only person I love.

"What do Gwen and Deniz know?" I ask, phrasing the question like one of the deadpan comments we used to trade on our early days on the research boat. Clara can't hide the shock that flashes across her face before she composes herself. Still, even in that laid back, ultra-confident demeanor I've come to love so much, it's clear how much my words mean to her.

"I imagine just about everything Charlie and Clara do," she replies, picking up her glass and sliding her leg against mine so my calf rests on her shin. Without a second thought, I pop my legs up under the table, crossing my ankles over her knee and leaning back against the padded booth.

"Then let's start with everything *you* know."

Her hand slips down, fingers gently pressing into my calf like she's reminding herself that I'm real.

"Alright, Pecas. Let's start there."

Epilogue One
Emily

Even after all this time, I really don't love the ocean. But Alice does, and I love her, so here I am.

Plus, I'm fairly certain that if I make up another excuse for not turning in data to my PhD advisor, she's going to cut me into microscopic, zooplankton-like pieces and use me as bait for the jellies. I barely convinced her to let me change my geographic focus to coastal Japan and the distribution of their native sea nettles.

Alice stares off at the horizon, her face serene yet deeply sad. Sometimes I think we're too close to where her mother died. My brave, beautiful girl's fears are much closer now than when she was on the other side of the Pacific.

"You okay?" I ask softly, knocking her foot with mine. She stirs out of her reprieve, blinking away the haze from her eyes. Despair and worry are still there though, and while I hate that she feels those things at all, I'm glad she doesn't hide them from me.

"Yeah, worried about what comes next," she admits with a shrug that's meant to be casual.

"Me too," I say, hoping it comforts her that we're both lost in this unknown.

Bea's been gone for about a week, the first time any of the Costa cousins have left Japan since the round trip flight Bea and I made to clean up the scene in Nesika Beach, pick up Ilya's iced over body, and gather both my and Alice's belongings. But Clara's informed us she's coming back tonight, and has requested everyone's presence at Bea's townhouse.

Seeing as I've been spending every moment not working or drafting my dissertation in Alice's bed, the sudden change in tone was a rude awakening. I've been teaching Alice more and more about The Syndicate, but it's felt distant and theoretical. I have a feeling everything will change tonight.

"Holy shit," Alice whispers, pointing directly at my ROV monitor. I whip my head around to watch the flickering screen, seeing absolutely nothing.

"Did you...?" I ask, my words trailing as Alice clambers out of her seat to move closer to the screen.

"I swear, watch," she whispers, like she's afraid she'll scare off whatever she saw. We hold our breath as our boat—much larger, more modern, and not nearly as soaked in memories as our last one—bobs gently on the waves. There's a flicker in the corner, and Alice gasps.

"Come on," she mutters, and something warm and liquid fills my chest as I watch her be so excited for my ridiculous, contrived research subject.

"Right there!"

And she's right.

Dozens of Japanese Sea Nettles filter through the water in front of the ROV, contracting their bells and propelling themselves through the deep. Their color is more muted and neutral than the Black Sea Nettles I was looking for on the other side of the ocean, but their long, delicate arms are so similar. I blink for a few moments before Alice slaps my leg with the back of her hand.

"Aren't you supposed to be taking notes or recording something? What kind of researcher are you?"

I can't stop myself from laughing as I shuffle through my bag for my notebook and data collection worksheets.

"I really didn't think we'd find them after only a few trips," I say, a little dumbfounded. "I mean I know they live in cold waters, but they've never been recorded this deep, as far as I'm aware."

"Emily, shut up and do your genius stuff," Alice says, not tearing her eyes away from the screen. "I want to dive with them."

"Absolutely not," I scoff, earning a glare from my favorite person. "They're venomous, Alice."

"I have the internet now, Emily," she bites back in a mocking tone, turning back to the screen to ogle at the cnidarians. "Their sting isn't usually fatal, unless you have an allergy."

I jot down our coordinates, the water temperature, depth, and pressure readings, and observations from the image blinking in front of us.

"I'm not telling you what you should or shouldn't do. But just because their stings aren't fatal doesn't mean they don't hurt like hell. Plus, I don't think it's humanly possible to dive over five hundred feet."

She grumbles something inaudible in response, and I try not to laugh at her disregard of caution. She really is the embodiment of the idea that fear isn't necessary.

After a few minutes of my scribbling and her oohing and ahhing, she finds a seat beside me and lays her head on my shoulder. Together, we watch the jellies and fish and other creatures of the deep float by, a universe humming hundreds of feet below us.

"So you found them. What's next?" Alice asks, interlacing her fingers with mine. I press my lips into her hair, savoring the way the sea magnifies her scent tenfold.

"Ideally, I'd collect samples of their nematocysts directly from their tentacles, or the stingers from their prey, so we can better understand how increasing water temperatures affect toxicity and lethality," I explain, remembering the night I spent brainstorming this research plan that would hopefully lead me to Alice. "But that's phase two. Right now, we observe them."

She hums, tipping her face up to soak in the sun's rays. I watch the light filter through her white-blonde hair, the underside freshly dyed pink.

I think about what Charlie said when he found Gwen. That the universe connects us to the people meant to change us. And he might be right. Maybe fate is inescapable.

But I like to think fate can be swayed. Because when Alice turns towards me, pressing her sun-warmed lips to mine, I know I would have always found my way to her. No matter how long the thread between us took to follow.

Epilogue Two
Alice

"You know what, I lied. I am afraid of something."

Emily chuckles behind me, but I can't hear it. This ear protection is particularly effective, but I can still feel her chest rumble because she's standing so close. She somehow moves even closer, pressing against my back and positioning her finger over mine on the trigger. With her other hand, she lifts one side of my earmuffs off.

"Sharks and rattlesnake poison are fine, but you're afraid of a little gun? I thought I was talking to the daughter of an infamous weapons runner."

I huff as she lets the earmuff snap back into place, already missing the feeling of her breath on my neck. Fifteen minutes ago, when I was watching her target practice, Emily's whispered voice in my ear would have gotten me halfway out of my clothes. Now, my lust is significantly dampened by the fear that I'm going to accidentally shoot her, or myself.

"May I remind you that I didn't even know my own clothing size until I faked my death? I wasn't exactly given a ton of weapons training," I bite back, trying to focus down the barrel at the target like she instructed.

Without speaking, Emily increases the pressure on my hand, tilting my wrist at a lower angle. She disengages the safety and taps the finger on the trigger with her own.

So I pull it.

And miss spectacularly.

If it wasn't for Emily's body bracing mine, I think the force of the shot would have blown my shoulder out of its socket. My bones rattle, a terrible zing racing up and down my frame like I'm a lamppost someone's taken a baseball bat to. I push the gun into Emily's hand and stumble away, ripping the ear protection off in the process.

"That wasn't too bad," Emily congratulates, her voice filled with genuine pride. How pathetic.

"I didn't get anywhere near that paper," I argue, gesturing wildly toward the hanging sheet with an outline of a human drawn on it. Not a bullet hole to be seen.

"Yeah, but you didn't kill either of us, so let's call it a success," she replies, and I hate that there's not a drop of condescension in her tone. She really is proud that I didn't shoot us.

"I never want to touch that thing again. I feel like I got clipped by a moving car," I grumble, rolling my shoulder out. "You said that was a small one."

"It is," she says with a shrug, engaging the safety and placing the weapon in its case. "But you're also small, and new at this. It takes practice to know how to absorb the blowback."

"Too bad I'll never learn. Oh well," I say. I know before she opens her mouth that there's no way I'm getting away with that.

"Sorry, Pecas. If you want to be a bonafide member of The Syndicate, you have to at least be able to handle a gun. And know how to disarm someone who's pointing one at you."

I know she's right. Over the past few weeks, as things have gotten more serious—both in the Costas' investigation and between Emily and I—I've learned more and more what it means to truly be a part of this family. Emily has been consistent in her offer to leave this life behind the moment her family is safe and mine is eliminated, but every insight I get into the work The Syndicate does only makes me want that for her less.

And for me as well.

We still haven't formally made a decision about what we'll do when this chapter of our lives is closed, if we survive. But one thing we know for certain is that we'll face that unknown together.

"And who says I want to do that?" I ask, easily slipping back into that slightly turned on mentality I occupied before I had to touch the wretched thing. Emily does that to me. Makes me feel safe—free to explore, to give in, to lose control, to *want*.

"You did, pretty girl," she replies, a sly smile on her lips as she locks the gun's case and beckons me toward her. "Two nights ago, if I remember correctly. *Make me, Emily. Make me yours.*"

"Hmm, I don't remember that," I lie, slowly making my way closer, dragging out my steps just to be a little obstinate. This dynamic is new within the last few weeks, but it's grown on both of us. Me fighting back, her putting me in my place. Usually by means of pleasure so overwhelming I beg for mercy she never gives.

It's a good dynamic.

"No?" she asks, her tone chiding and patronizing and soothing all the zinging in my bones. She slips her fingers into the waistband of my long, flowy skirt, tugging me into her until my chest is pressed to hers and I have to tilt my chin far up to meet her gaze. "Do I need to remind you?"

"Remind me of what?" I push, slipping my arms around her waist and dragging my nails up and down her spine. "Of how good it feels when you make me?"

There's a flash of something primal and needy in her eyes,

and she flips us so my lower back is pressed to the table, her hands skating down my sides and to my ass.

"Is that what you want, Pecas?" she asks, lifting my thighs so she can slide me up on the metal table. Even through my skirt, the cold surface bites my flesh, more intense because of how hot my skin feels. "For me to remind you that I know your body better than you do?"

She forces my knees further apart before I can respond, threading her fingers through the hair at the name of my neck and tilting my face up so she can look in my eyes.

"Yes, please," I admit, the flood of adrenaline rushing through my veins more powerful than anything I've ever experienced. Emily doesn't move, doesn't even breathe. Her eyes scan my face, looking for something she won't find. She's always so careful, every time we play on this edge. Her dedication to making sure I have as much control in my life as possible extends even to when I want to give it up.

And in this moment, I *do* want to let go of the control I always so desperately seek. To know someone wholeheartedly dedicated to my pleasure is deciding how I find it. I want to beg her to stop, knowing she won't. I want her to force me to take what she tells me I deserve.

I want to feel inherently safe with the only person I could possibly trust this much.

"What's your safe word?" she asks, so very still, her body nearly vibrating with the effort of holding herself back. It's intoxicating, knowing how badly she wants to make me come. How much she craves me.

"クラゲ," I reply, forcing her careful, controlled expression to break as she laughs.

"English, Spanish, or Russian please," she says, kneading the base of my neck with her thumb and forefinger. "Only give me your safe word in a language at least one of us is fluent in."

"Since when is that a rule?" I ask, being difficult on purpose, because she loves it. She doesn't ever punish me for it either. More like she encourages it, finding new ways to make me tumble over even higher cliffs of pleasure when I push her buttons.

"Since when do you question my rules?" she shoots back, pulling my hair at the root, forcing my back to arch and my blood to heat another couple of degrees.

"All the time," I say with a teasing smile. In response, she grabs my hip and yanks my ass to the edge of the table so her legs are pressed right between my thighs. Her mouth is millimeters from mine when she repeats the question.

"What is your safe word?"

I think about being difficult once more, just to see how far I can push her, but I'm already too on edge. And I know she needs to hear that we both know the rules and are on the same page.

"Jellyfish," I reply, earning myself the softest, lightest brush of her lips against mine. I chase it, even though her grip in my hair keeps me from what I want.

"And what happens if you say no? Or stop?" She keeps her other hand planted firmly on the table beside me. I want it over my mouth. Around my throat. Between my thighs.

"You won't listen," I answer, my eyes dropping to where her chest rises and falls. It feels so perfect, knowing how badly we need each other. How obvious it is to both of us.

"What is the only way to get me to stop touching you?" she asks, being more explicit than she ever has before. It only makes this hotter. Because I know she's going to push me to my limit, and I can't fucking wait.

"Saying my safeword. In English, Russian, or Spanish," I say, being as thorough as I can so she knows I'm taking this seriously.

"You're sure about this?" she asks, her eyes softer now, hesitating slightly. I raise my hand to her forearm, dragging my fingers from wrist to elbow, needing to feel her skin under mine.

"I trust you, Emily," I whisper, wrapping my fingers around her arm and squeezing. "I love you."

It's not the first time I've said it. That came when she took me on a private whale-watching tour off the eastern coast of Choshi, as she leaned over the railing even though she was clearly terrified, and asked me to tell her about the migratory patterns of whales on this side of the Pacific.

But each time I say it, she looks like I've sewn the world together for her. She gets the same expression when I play viola. I imagine I look the same when she's brave for me, and when she finds ways to let me choose.

"I love you, Pecas," she says, pressing her lips to my forehead and breathing deeply.

And then her grip tightens at the base of my neck, and everything changes.

Emily angles my head up again and seals her lips to mine, kissing me like it's the last one before the end of the world. I need little encouragement to open my mouth, allowing her access to whatever part of me she wants.

Her other hand travels slowly up my leg, pushing my skirt up until it's bunched at my waist. Each inch closer to my pussy pulls broken cries and moans from my lips, muffled against her mouth. I need more—I *always* need more with her—and I feel my hips lift of their own volition, seeking her touch.

She doesn't tease because she doesn't have to. Each touch makes my blood pump faster, and I can already feel how wet I am before she cups me over my underwear.

"Always so ready for me," she murmurs as she pulls her lips from mine, keeping one hand in my hair so she can control where I look. Right now, she makes sure my eyes are locked on hers as she grinds the heel of her palm against my clit. I whimper, already raising my hips against her hand, seeking out more pressure.

"Emily, please," I whine, the angle limiting my ability to move against her. All the fight I had a few moments ago has dissolved like sugar in water, and I'll beg if that's what gets her to give me what I need.

"You have to be quiet for me, baby. Can you do that?" she asks, pressing her fingers against my entrance through the fabric. I choke out another frustrated cry, my eyes drifting closed as I focus on chasing that feeling only she can give me.

"Apparently not," she laughs. Without warning, she slides her fingertips under the waistband of my underwear, stepping back to pull them down my legs. "This is a private bay, but we don't want anyone else at the range to hear you, do we?"

Exposed, with my legs still spread for her, I try to find the words to answer her. But before I get the chance, Emily balls up my underwear and taps my chin with her knuckle.

"Open."

And because I want her to choose for me, I do.

There's a little initial panic when breathing gets harder, my mouth stuffed full of cotton, but Emily watches me carefully, inhaling through her nose like an example for my overstimulated brain to follow. As soon I'm breathing evenly again, Emily shoves my skirt up, pressing my thighs open.

"There you go, Pecas," she placates, staring at my pussy like she owns it. "Now you can beg and scream and cry all you want."

The sob that wrenches from my throat when she touches my clit is muffled, but it still lights a fire in her eyes. Emily wastes no time, her fingers moving easily slicked with the undeniable evidence of how much I need her. So badly I could cry, and she knows it. I beg for more, even though she can't possibly understand my words. But Emily could always read my body, and the way I'm rocking my hips against her hand, demanding more from her slow, gentle movements, is clear.

A finger slips into my entrance, and I grip the edge of the table, using every ounce of leverage I have to chase the feeling. Usually Emily talks so much when she fucks me, telling me how perfect or beautiful or brave or good I am, but she's silent now. So focused on where we're connected, her pupils blown as she picks up the pace.

The sound of my muffled cries and my soaked pussy echoing off the metal and concrete of this room are obscene, reflecting my own pleasure back at me and ratcheting it up tenfold. Emily slips a second, and then third finger inside me, but it's not only the fullness that pushes me closer and closer to the edge. It's the way she fucks me roughly, like I can take it, like she knows I'm not fragile or breakable. The pleasure teeters on the verge of pain, a razor-thin edge that we dance on together as I meet her thrust for thrust.

My orgasm slams through me, tears leaking from my eyes, cries stifled by the fabric in my mouth as the pleasure rolls through me over and over again. My eyes are clenched shut, but Emily grips the base of my neck harder, and they fly open to see her watching me fall apart.

"More, pretty girl."

My pussy is so sensitive and overstimulated that I shake my head, and Emily briefly lets go to yank the underwear from my mouth.

"Something to say, Pecas?" she asks, still pounding into me, the waning orgasm transforming into the beginnings of a new one, building in my core all over again.

"It's too much," I whine, trying my hardest to keep my

voice low. Emily's answering smile would be cruel if there wasn't so much adoration in it.

"I don't think it's enough," she says, pushing my shoulder back gently so I'm laying flat on the long, metal table. At the edge, she uses the hand not fucking me into oblivion to press into my thigh, holding me wide open for her.

Unbelievably, she picks up her pace even more, sweat beading at her hairline as she fucks me harder and faster than I knew I could handle. My skin vibrates with need, the table under me warm and slick with my own sweat as I arch into the feeling.

I know I'm chanting *I can't I can't I can't*, but the words feel far away. Everything's floaty and buzzing as I take what Emily gives, This time the orgasm builds slower, but she doesn't give me an inch, fucking me like I can take anything.

She grabs my hand. Moves it to my chest. Guides my fingers to roll my own nipple between them.

And I fall apart like the world is ending.

Every inch of my body feels electrified, frying my brain cells into oblivion as I come on her fingers. Emily's free hand covers my mouth, but I can't feel bad for crying out when she makes me feel like this. So free, so unbreakable, so perfect.

Finally, she starts to slow her movements. She gathers my limp frame, tucking my underwear into her back pocket as she lifts me into her arms, murmuring praise into my hair as she kisses me.

I know we're not done. That Emily will probably give me water and a little rest, take us back to my apartment so she can finish what she started. And even though I can already feel my heart rate picking up at the thought, I savor this moment. Broken and whole with the only person who makes me feel unbreakable.

Acknowledgments

Dearest Gentle Reader! You made it through book three!

Thank you to every single one of you for reading Alice and Emily's story. This is my first ever sapphic book, and to say I was nervous when I began writing is an understatement of epic proportions. As a queer person, reading stories that represent the love I experience has always been a source of immense joy and comfort, but writing one was a whole new world. I owe my queer friends who dev/alpha/sensitivity read and edited this book my life, because you trusted and helped me along the way, and I'm forever grateful. And to the sapphic readers who have gotten to the last few pages of *Waters*, I love you very much. Thank you for creating community with me in this beautiful bookish space.

As I've said in every acknowledgements section I've written since I've begun publishing, I appreciate that working on my team isn't the easiest process. I'm anxious and in constant need of validation (pisces, lol), and sometimes I tell you I will have chapters to you by Wednesday and they certainly do *not* come on Wednesday. So I endlessly appreciate the people who have stayed in my corner through my writing career, especially in this book that means so much to me.

As always, to Rose. My forever-dev. My bestie. Simultaneously the least and most patient person I know. Thanks for being here three (well, four if we count the book we can't talk about yet) books in. Please don't leave me.

Thousands upon thousands of thanks to Erica and Cas. Not only for alpha reading this book and answering the question "is this gay enough" five thousand times, but also for greatly expanding my knowledge of sapphic music during this process. My least pisces trait is having almost zero knowledge of music, and you've multiplied that ten fold. I appreciate you always.

To Vanessa! First, for fixing my less that stellar Spanish. But also for breathing life into Emily's backstory. The beautiful nuance you brought to Emily's word choice, memories, and interactions was beyond helpful. And you chose Emily's nickname for Alice! I'll be forever grateful to you for *Pecas*.

Oh Heather. My editing queen. My fellow jellyfish lover (and hater of the word cnidarian). Thank you for your patience with my incredibly slow writing pace and my inability to notice when I'm repeating the same word 70 times in 3 pages. I wish you could edit my thoughts before I speak them out loud.

Amanda, every time you send me a cover and it's basically perfect on the first round, I don't know what to do with myself. Thank you for knowing exactly how to bring these moody horny murder books to life. One more to go!

I'd also love to shout out the artists who I book for literally every single book I write because I'm so desperately in love with how they bring my characters to life. To Elaine (@pixilaine) for my character art and Roise (@rosiefables) for my NSFWs, thank you for always taking me back on as a client. From a person with aphantasia who cannot see these characters in my mind at all, you'll never know how much I appreciate having them in front of me to reference and adore while I'm writing.

And of course, to Erin. Since the time I've started writing this book, you have designed tablescapes, PA'd at events, packed PR boxes, created tarot card art, redesigned my marketing materials like ten thousand times, and done a billion other things. You're more than a best friend. I love you to the moon.

And again, to my readers. Staying with an author through an entire series is a huge ask, and y'all have made it ¾ of the way through. I hope you stick around to see how the Syndicate of Fate series ends with Bea's story...

About the Author

Rae Douglas (they/she/he) is an author and emergency manager from the San Francisco Bay. They love writing stories about mutual obsession, family trauma, healthy BDSM and kink, and friends who know platonic love is just as valuable as romantic love. They have lived all over the United States, from Los Angeles to D.C. to Branson, and love road tripping as much as possible. In their free time, they can be found in a natural history museum, at a baseball game, or on a whale watching excursion. They can be found at @authorraedouglas on all platforms.